Relationships Can Be Murder

Jane DiLucchio

D1738194

New Victoria Publishers

Norwich, Vermont

Published by New Victoria Publishers Inc., PO Box 27 Norwich, Vt.
05055, a Feminist Literary and Cultural Organization founded in 1976.

Cover photo by Kelly Kissel
Cover design concept by Nola Lunstedt
Back cover author photo by Sue Stimpson

Printed and bound the USA
First printing 2005

Library of Congress Cataloging-in-Publication Data

DiLucchio, Jane, 1953-
  Relationships can be murder / by Jane DiLucchio.
     p. cm.
  ISBN 1-892281-25-2
  1. Women television journalists--Crimes against--Fiction. 2. Los
Angeles (Calif.)--Fiction. 3. Lesbians--Fiction. I. Title.

  PS3604.I4635R45 2005
  813'.6--dc22

                                                    2005013336

To my mother, Helen, who taught me to love a mystery.

To Serra's Sisters, for their unconditional support and encouragement.

To my art group, for instigating new creative endeavors.

To Sue, for everything.

Prelude

The woman lay sprawled on her right side across the damask-covered couch, one arm flung above her head, the other draped across her stomach. A dressing gown was half-drawn around her, exposing one long leg and most of her ample cleavage. Blonde hair curled around her face.

Two Tiffany lamps lit the room, one on an end table and the other, shade cracked, sitting on the floor. The lamps cast a rainbow of colors across the woman and the sheaves of paper strewn over the blues and greens of the plush Persian rug in the living room. The framed awards and letters on the wall to the right of the couch were no longer the least bit parallel to each other. The brass and glass bookshelf that usually stood opposite the couch lay on its side, its contents adding to the disorder on the floor.

The oak rolltop desk in the far corner of the room sat exposed, its drawers open and empty. The computer normally hidden within its recesses was on, but the screen was blank.

On the glass coffee table in front of the couch were two glasses and a bottle of Dom Perignon in a crystal ice bucket. The bucket had only a few ice chips left in it, and the moisture from the outside had formed a beaded circle of water on the tabletop.

The disarray would normally have perturbed the woman greatly. In fact, she would have been extremely uncomfortable to have anyone see the condo, or herself, in this condition.

However, a deep concave dent on the back of her head had ended all her mundane concerns of embarrassment.

Chapter 1

Dee DelValle slid through the crowd of smokers outside Club Sheba and dug in the back pocket of her jeans for her ID. The sardine can atmosphere of a Saturday night at the West Hollywood hot spot made maneuvering difficult. The bouncer at the door illuminated her driver's license with a flashlight, then motioned her in. The conversation and drumbeat were at about the same high intensity, and in inverse proportion to the amount of light inside the bar.

An irrational desire to light a cigarette flashed through Dee's mind. Doubly irrational considering she did not smoke and hated the smell of cigarettes. But she hated even more the bureaucrats of California telling people what they could and could not do. However, since she was here for a celebration, she decided to hold off on her act of civil disobedience until another time.

As Dee stood still and waited for her eyes to adjust, she heard her name being called. She wove her way through the lounging singles and dancing couples, carefully juggling a gaily festooned box around the crush of people. Both she and the present arrived safely at three tables which had been dragged together into a close grouping.

"Howdy, Dee!" A tall, well-developed woman jumped up and hugged Dee.

"Hey, Tully!" Dee flashed a megawatt grin at her best friend. She set the box on one of the tables and then leaned back for a second look at Tully's wavy shoulder-length locks. "Red tonight?"

"Please. Auburn. With fiery highlights." Tallulah Bouchart's hair was never the same color for more than a month or so. Dee suspected Tully considered it but another palette on which to use her creative talents. To Dee's mind those color variations combined with Tully's hooded eyes, hooked nose, and full lips made her distinctively attractive.

Plopping her slight frame into the tiny chair, Dee looked around at the other eight chairs and asked," Where's everyone else?"

"Late. Or we're really early. Doesn't matter. I asked Jenny to pick Felicia up and make sure they get here very late, so the surprise will work."

"Does this mean that Jenny has finally noticed Felicia's rather ardent interest in her?"

Tully shook her head. "Jenny is kind of a shy filly. She's really slow on the uptake when it comes to women being interested in her. However, a little assigned together time can't hurt."

"Why you little matchmaker you. Anyway, I still say this is a weird place to have a birthday party." Dee had to almost shout into Tully's ear to be heard. "Not much chance to socialize."

"True. But the liquor's nearby and the dance floor is open. What more could one ask of life?"

Dee shook her head at her friend, a not unusual occurrence. "So where's you amour du jour?"

"None on tap tonight. Thought I'd check out the local talent." Tully waggled her eyebrows and grinned, bringing out a dazzling display of dimples. "What about you? Seeing anybody since you-know-who?"

"You know I've sworn off women. I'm a slow learner, but not that slow." Dee looked around for a server. "Have you ordered anything yet?"

"A veritable repast of delights: nachos, chicken fingers, fried zucchini. And a gin and tonic. At least that's the first course."

Dee rolled her eyes at her friend. Tully could, and did, eat anything and never budged beyond her rather robust size. Dee's genetic heritage had a decided tendency towards fat, a tendency she fought with great diligence. "I just want ice water. But I may as well be in the Gobi desert." She waved her arm at a waitress who passed by without looking in their direction.

The music shifted to a soft, romantic tune. The dance floor filled with women, bodies pressed tightly together, legs as well as arms intertwining. The two friends were suddenly able to converse without yelling.

"So, good buddy," Tully asked, "are you going to make it these last few weeks until summer?"

Dee shrugged. "The kids are antsy, the principal's crazed, and the Board of Ed is their usual unreasonable selves. A normal May for a teacher." She added, "Of course my mood swings the last few months haven't helped."

"Premenopausal or affair backlash?"

"Losing Evie over my unleashed libido didn't help my teaching style any."

Tully snorted. "You knew when you started up with that blonde bimbo."

"Yeah, yeah. I don't want to rehash this. Evie rubbed my nose in it enough."

"But you're so rarely foolish. It's such a delight to be able to point out what an ass you were." Tully's eyes twinkled.

Dee grimaced. "No need for you to join in the fun. Evie made certain that I was more acutely aware of my deficiencies than any human being ever has been in all of recorded history."

"Knowing Ms. Taylor's facility with words, I am sure you don't need me to re-emphasize your appalling lack of judgment, "Tully said.

Dee said, "Nope. But even you've got to admit that Sheila is good looking, talented and famous as well as self-centered. Of course, having your picture plastered on billboards and the sides of RTD buses all over town has got to have some sort of effect on your self-esteem. Add to that two Emmys for reporting and more awards for best local news anchor and you have somewhat justified fat head."

"Television awards," Tully snorted. "Honors among thieves."

"Now, now. Don't bite the hand that partially feeds you."

A brunette clad in tight jeans and a cotton top appeared at their table with three steaming plates and a tall, icy glass. Tully paid the bill and gave the waitress a healthy tip and a long, slow, dimpled smile. Having experienced Tully's effect on women, Dee could see that she'd have to exert herself if she wanted the waitress to acknowledge her existence, let alone take her drink order.

Waving her hand in front of the brunette's face, Dee requested some bottled water. The waitress nodded, but her look slipped back to Tully and she gave her a slight smile before leaving.

Dee knew that she, herself, was not a beauty. However her heart-shaped face, wide green eyes, thick lashes, and snub nose had brought enough favorable responses from others that her ego was fairly strong. She sighed at Tully and said, "Women never ignore me until I get around you. When you look at them, they always look back. How do you manage?"

Tully picked up a chicken finger and swirled it in the sweet and sour sauce, "If it weren't for some woman who smiled back at me fifteen years ago, I'd still be on the wrong side of the fence. I infinitely prefer this side. And I love showing other women what they might be missing."

"Tallulah Bouchart, you are a menace to all the women in the world. If they only knew."

Tully just continued to grin as she licked the sauce off the fried bit of chicken breast.

"Dee! Tully!" A booming voice carried across several yards of noise to reach the women. Turning, they saw a tall plump woman bullying her way through the crowd. Within seconds Nancy Yegarian was hurling her bulk into one of the tiny bar chairs which groaned in protest. "Did you catch the news tonight?" Her excited voice blasted through the music.

"I try not to," Dee replied. "What's up? Have we invaded another country or something?"

"Nah, nothing like that. There's been a murder."

Tully snorted. "This is L.A. A murder is not exactly page one, stop-the-presses news."

Nancy shook her head. "This one is. Someone killed Sheila Shelbourne."

Dee leaned against her metallic purple Hyundai in the Club Sheba parking lot, arms folded around herself. She felt an internal chill which had nothing to do with the cool of the late spring evening. As she inhaled, her chest tightened and goose bumps crawled her arms.

She wasn't aware of Tully's approach until she felt an arm wrap around her shoulders. Dee leaned into Tully's shoulder and let her friend cradle her.

Reluctant to emerge from the safe, warm cocoon, Dee said into Tully's shoulder, "I know you never liked her."

"You're right. And her being dead doesn't change the fact that she was a lying, cheating slut who hurt you and about every other woman she ever crossed paths with. But that still doesn't give anybody the right to kill her." Her voice gentled. "And it doesn't help you deal with someone you loved being dead."

"I never loved her. Not really." Dee emerged from the crook of Tully's arm and leaned against the car once more. "I guess somehow that makes it worse. I went to bed with her because she was sexy and exciting and beautiful and famous. And I really didn't care about her as a person at all. Good grief," she added, rubbing the back of her neck, "I might as well be a man."

Tully scoffed, "Five-feet, four, barely one twenty five pounds soaking wet, and you wear your heart on your sleeve. Some macho punk you'd be."

"I bow to your superior knowledge of the species," Dee took a deep breath. "Be that as it may, I still can't believe— Who would?"

"Kill her?" Tully finished Dee's thought. She craned her head to look into the night. Only the moon and a few of the strongest stars were visible in the brightly lit Los Angeles sky. "Who would kill Sheila? Probably a lot of people if they knew her true character. All those adoring television viewers who hung on her every report. All her fans in the lesbian community who thought she walked on water because she was out and she condescended to mingle openly in the community. All those women who left their lovers or whose lovers left them because of Sheila Shelbourne. I guess the police will have close to a million good, solid suspects."

Dee studied her friend in the light of the street lamp. "I never knew you hated her that much. What did she ever do to you?"

"To me? Nothing." Tully shrugged. "To my friends…" She raised her eyebrows. "Anyway, mi amiga, no matter how anticlimactic it is, the birthday girl will be arriving soon. Do you feel like coming in or should I make your excuses? You know Felicia loves you and would understand."

"I think I'll take you up on that. Somehow, I'm not in a party mood. I feel like binging and then sleeping until noon."

"You sure you're OK to drive home?"

"Yeah. Don't worry. What else could happen?"

Chapter 2

The banging on her front door caused Dee to pause mid-bite. The whipped cream and fudge topping slid off the vanilla ice cream and mingled with the strawberry sauce and the remaining banana in the cardboard dish. When a second round of pounding began, she placed the half-empty Baskin-Robbins container on the glass of her coffee table and trudged to the door.

"Yes?" she called through the closed portal as she snapped on the front door light and looked out the fish-eye glass at the man and woman on her front step.

The woman wore black pants, a crisp white shirt, and a deep blue blazer. She stepped towards the peephole. Flipping open an ID case she said, "LAPD."

Dee rested her forehead against the coolness of the wooden door. She unlocked the three-inch deadbolt and opened the door with the safety chain still attached. "May I see your identification again?" she asked the two figures on the step. She studied the two laminated cards and shields then released the chain and beckoned them in.

"Sorry about being so untrusting, but you hear things." Dee shrugged and let her voice drift away. She switched on two tall torch lamps. "What can I do for you, Detective...?"

"Quinn," the tall woman replied as she brought her dark eyes back from surveying the room and stared straight into Dee's face. The laugh lines around the detective's eyes and the streaks of gray in otherwise black hair made Dee estimate the policewoman to be in her late thirties. Quinn's half decade of seniority added to Dee's feelings of insecurity.

"And this is my partner, Detective Pierce." Alex Pierce, with his sandy hair, crew cut, and bright blue eyes seemed younger and friendlier that his cohort. Dee ventured a smile at him, but he merely nodded in return as he opened his notebook and took out a pen from his suit jacket's breast pocket.

Gina Quinn glanced down at the melting banana split. "Sorry to interrupt your dessert, but we're looking into an incident and we're hoping you can give us some information." The detective paused but all she received in return was a blank stare from Dee. "You are Diega DelValle?" pronouncing it 'DelValley.'

"Del vie-yay." Dee corrected. "It's Spanish." She waved the detectives into two wicker chairs and reclaimed her place on the love seat.

The cane on the chair squeaked as Quinn settled herself. Opening her own notebook, she leafed through several pages before asking, "Could you tell us where you were yesterday from about noon until seven o'clock?"

"I presume this has to do with Sheila Shelbourne?"

Quinn raised one already arched eyebrow. "Why do you think this is about Ms. Shelbourne's death?"

"Forgive me for jumping to conclusions, but the news of Sheila's death has been hard to miss. You're asking me about yesterday, and that's when she was killed. And the reports are calling it a murder, not a suicide or accident. Plus, you're LAPD. This is Burbank. Not exactly your jurisdiction. If this isn't about Sheila, I can't imagine what."

Dee brought her legs up onto the love seat and crossed them into a yoga position. It was as close as she could get to a fetal position without seeming too obvious. "If I had to guess, I'd say her murder didn't happen in the course of a robbery or you wouldn't be checking out Sheila's acquaintances. Am I close?"

Quinn and Pierce regarded her in silence. Finally, Quinn

said, "You are right that we are investigating the death of Ms. Shelbourne. However, the circumstances around her death are not something we can discuss at this moment." She leaned back in the chair. Her head topped the high back of the wicker. "I take it you knew Sheila Shelbourne personally."

Dee paused. "Yes, I know—knew her."

"How would you describe your relationship with her?" Quinn asked.

"Stupid."

"Your relationship was stupid or was that a comment directed towards me?" Quinn face held a hint of a smile.

Dee blushed. "I meant I was stupid for even having any kind of relationship with her."

Pierce cleared his throat. "Was this a…romantic relationship?"

"No, it was a sexual relationship. There wasn't much romance to it at all."

"Was this a current love affair?" This time the question came from Quinn, so Dee was uncertain how to focus her responses.

"No. It ended about a month ago. Amicably, I might add."

"From whose point of view?" Back to Pierce.

"Both of ours. Look, it was never serious for either of us. It was no big deal when it ended."

"Then why were you stupid to get involved with her?" Quinn raised her eyebrows at Dee.

Dee shifted on the small couch, aware that the remains of her ice cream splurge were turning to curds and whey. Relieved that she'd only have to jog an extra two miles instead of four since she didn't finish the second half of the caloric indulgence, she drew her mind back to the detective's question. Sighing she said, "I was already involved with someone. I'd been seeing her for about a year when I started up with Sheila. Anyway, my fling with Sheila ended my relationship. That was the stupid part."

"Who was this other woman?" Detective Pierce picked up

the ball this time.

"She really had nothing to do with Sheila. If there was anyone she'd want to kill, it'd be me."

"Could we have her name?"

"Why?"

His colorless voice responded predictably, "Just routine."

Dee glanced away then came back to his blue eyes. "Evelyn. Taylor. She lives on Elm in Pasadena."

"When did you last see Ms. Shelbourne?" Detective Quinn asked.

Dee hesitated. "See Sheila? About three weeks ago. Right after we decided to call it quits."

Quinn changed direction. "During your relationship, did you ever meet any of Ms. Shelbourne's friends?"

Dee just shook her head.

"Can you think of anyone who might have ill feelings towards her?"

Thinking of Tully's reaction to such a question, Dee had to work to keep a smile from her face. "All I can tell you is I didn't kill her and I don't know who did."

Quinn jotted a notation in her notebook. "So, would you tell us where you were yesterday from noon until seven?"

Dee sighed. "Persistent, aren't you?" When no response came, she continued. "Yesterday. Friday. Well that makes the first part easy. I teach and I was in class from twelve until three. Then I was in my classroom preparing next week's lessons until about four or four-thirty. After that, I ran some errands and stopped by the grocery store and bought some veggies to make a stir-fry for dinner. I got home about six, changed, made dinner, and was probably eating around seven." Dee paused. "Sounds exciting, doesn't it?"

"Ma'am," Pierce's low rumble broke through the silence, "did anyone see you in your classroom after school or did anyone come over before or during your dinner?"

Dee raised her eyebrows at the man. "Do you mean can anyone verify my alibi? No."

"Alibi?" Quinn's voice held a question.

"What would you call it?"

Quinn glanced at her partner of six years and nodded. They both closed their notebooks and stood. "Thank you for your cooperation. We may be back to talk with you again. In the meantime, if you think of anything you'd like to add to your statement, please give me a call." With that, she handed Dee a business card and headed for the door.

After Dee watched the two police detectives get into their black Ford and drive off, she leaned her back against the inside of her front door and took a deep breath. Steeling herself, she reached for the telephone. The call was answered on the second ring.

"Evie? It's Dee. Don't hang up. I need to talk to you."

Dee dropped the phone into its cradle and sighed. Breaking the news to Evelyn was no picnic, but it was better than hearing from her after the police arrived on her doorstep.

As she threw away the unappetizing remains of her ice cream binge, she contemplated her next move. She knew that she had been technically honest. She also knew she had tried to escape deeper involvement in the whole nightmare by carefully wording her answers.

She figured the police would be back, especially if they found out about one of her errands Friday night. She also figured they would be less cordial the second time around. She just couldn't conceive of how to get around the visit. Hiring a lawyer was always a possibility, but, regardless of the letter of the American justice system, that seemed an act of guilt.

Calling her parents was never an option. Dee knew she'd get the lecture about how the DelValle name could be traced back seven generations to the Spanish land grants in California. They would be appalled at anyone in their family being so common as to be part of a criminal investigation.

Dee wandered her quiet house. The decorator-selected art and furniture were the same as always, but she drew no more comfort from them than she would a walk through an Ethan Allen showroom. When they were together, Evie had urged her to adopt a pet, grow a garden, create her own home. Dee just wasn't interested. The house had rarely felt lonely, but tonight the silence and darkness and rootlessness combined to enhance her fear and vulnerability.

The shrill ringing of the telephone caused the goose bumps between her shoulder blades to triple. With more eagerness to stop the annoying sound than to talk with anyone, Dee snatched the instrument before it could ring a second time. Tully's Texas twang filled her ear.

"Just checking up on you. Everybody was concerned."

"Thanks. I'm just deciding whether I'm better off throwing myself on the mercy of the court or getting an Uzi and shooting Sheila to death all over again for causing me this grief."

"Actually, you'd be shooting her for the first time."

"Huh?"

"Technically, you'd have to bash her one if you were doing it all over again. Of course, if you wanted to do something original—"

"Bash? You mean like in 'blunt object'?"

"Yeah. But they're not saying what kind or how many times or anything else. Playing it very close to the vest. But why are you planning a courtroom plea? You been up to something?"

Dee slumped into the love seat and propped her heels on the coffee table. "Actually, I just had what should have been a stimulating conversation with a good-looking woman. Unfortunately she had a man with her. And even more unfortunately, she works for the LAPD."

"Shit. How did they connect you so fast? There have got to be a million women in Sheila's little black book."

"Well, DelValle is pretty close to the beginning of the alphabet. Or maybe someone knew we had dated recently. I don't know, but it ticks me off to feel so helpless."

"You, my dear, are many things. But helpless is not one of them." Tully paused in thought. "Did the cops seem like they were testing the waters or were they ready to arrest you?"

"Well, they didn't warn me to get a lawyer or not to leave town or anything, but they did ask for Evie's name."

Tully's laugh exploded in Dee's ear. "I'm sure they'll get an education as to the foibles and failing of one Sheila Shelbourne from Ms. Taylor."

"What worries me are her list of my foibles and failings."

"Not to worry. Evie is one level-headed lady. She won't blow off steam about you in front of the police. And I hope to God she's not stupid enough to make them suspect her."

"Evie would never hurt a fly. If she were going to kill either one of us, she would have done it right then and there, not six weeks later. She'd never—"

"Much as I hate to interrupt this passionate defense of the woman who dumped you, I just got a brilliant idea."

"Oh, lord," Dee moaned. She was well aware of Tully's impulsive tendencies. That did not mean she approved of them.

"Oh ye of little faith. Listen, the police are barking up the wrong tree. Why?"

"I'm not sure which tree they are barking up, so how do I know why?"

"Honey, they all but peed on your roots. Now why you? This is a celebrity case and the police are going to be under a lot of pressure to solve this one and solve it fast. And you're easy."

Dee bridled. "That's just a rumor Nancy started to get back at me. I'm just as discriminating as your average lesbian."

"Which isn't saying much. And is beside the point. I mean you're an easy target. And why are you an easy target?" Tully rushed on before Dee could try to answer. "They don't know our community. They don't understand our culture. So that's why they'll pick on you and that's why we have to be the ones."

"The ones? We? Who killed her?" Dee's forehead creased as

she tried to follow her friend's rather wavy line of thought.

"No, not kill her. To solve it."

"Solve what?"

"Haven't you been listening? Sheila's murder. We know the people involved. We know the inside story. And we know you didn't do it. That's a lot more than the police know. So we've got to do our civic duty." Tully's tone carried decisively over the phone line. "I'll be over tomorrow morning at nine."

Dee massaged at the ache that was growing in her head. "Why are you coming over tomorrow at nine?"

"To pick you up, of course. The game's afoot, dear Sherlock. We've got a murderer to catch.

Chapter 3

"Tell me again how you think this is going to work." Dee sipped her Red Zinger through the tiny opening in the plastic top of the cardboard cup. The cool breeze whipped her hair and brought tears to her eyes. Tully's Jeep was a true Army vehicle—no sides and only a canvas top fastened to the windshield. A speed bump on the Burbank side street leading to Olive Avenue caused Dee to grip the armrest with one hand while holding the hot tea a safe distance from her body.

Tully shook her head. "Did Lacey have to explain everything twice to Cagney? Now, listen. What could be more reasonable than to start with Sheila's work? And what better way to check out Channel 8 than to drop by and visit our dear friend and recent birthday celebrant, Felicia?"

"Who just happens to be the make-up artist for the news show. That I got. What I don't get is what ploy we're going to use to get us on to the lot not to mention getting people to talk to us."

"You have no imagination." Tully fished in her back pocket while dangling her left wrist over the steering wheel. Luckily Olive Avenue was a straight shot at that point. She slid a plastic coated piece of colored cardboard free and waved it at Dee. "Our pass! I called Felicia and she's going to leave our names at Gate 3. And Jenny will join us so we can split up the interviews."

Dee snatched the pass and examined it closely. "This is a press pass. Where in the world...? Did Felicia...? And how are we supposed to…?"

"Given your evident inability to articulate complete sentences, our questioning the Channel 8 News Team may be more of a chore than I thought. Maybe I need a new partner. Do you think Jane Marple would be willing to hop the Concorde from St. Mary Mead?"

"I think we can safely assume she's retired by now. And if she weren't," Dee added, placing her empty tea container on the floor of the jeep between her feet, "partnering with you would send her there."

Tully swung a wide left into a side entry of the Channel 8 lot. As Tully flashed the pass and gave their names to the guard in the small booth, Dee glanced at the Pathways Studios production lot. Tall, gray buildings shadowed narrow concrete avenues between them. Large, flat sound studios slathered with the same plaster gray sides. Only large numbers painted on the sides of the buildings gave any hint of differentiation.

"Isn't it amazing," Dee said as Tully pulled the Jeep into the assigned spot, "that a business whose purpose is to creatively entertain, houses itself in such dull and boring buildings?"

"Dull exteriors sometimes hide fascinating interiors."

"Pronouncing profundities, are we?"

"Indubitably, my dear Watson."

"I thought you hated Sherlock."

"Well, he is a bit dry. But he comes in handy at times."

Tully led the way along the walkway to the right. Dee paused to throw her cardboard cup away before they entered building 12, home of the Channel 8 News Team LA.

Dee knew Hollywood liked to bill itself as the movie capital of the world, but, in her mind, Burbank should at least be listed as co-star. She had seen Burbank change from a quiet bedroom community for the Lockheed Aircraft Corporation to a media mecca. Universal Studios touched its borders. Warner Brothers and Disney studios both called Burbank their home, as did the television studios of NBC and Channel 8.

Since both Dee and Tully had visited Felicia on the set before, they had no problem winding their way along the non-delineated paths, past frantic people on foot and bike carrying everything from stacks of computer print-outs to cables to coffee. The relative sanity of the make-up area seemed a relief.

"Hey, girlfriends!" Felicia's smile gleamed from her milk chocolate face as she hugged both Tully and Dee at the same time, not an easy feat considering the five-inch difference in their heights.

Seeing as Dee got the arm with the scissors on the end, she untangled herself carefully. "Hey, yourself. And thanks for letting us come."

Felicia knotted her hands on her hips. "What kind of friend would let those police accuse you of murder and not do a simple little thing like this to help?"

"Well, they didn't exactly accuse—"

"Now, never you mind. We'll straighten them out. In fact, I was just telling them how wrong they are about you."

"You mean they've already been here?" Tully asked.

"Still are." Felicia waved her scissor hand, "Somewhere around."

Dee reached out and extracted the scissors from Felicia's left hand. "You're making me nervous. Someone could get hurt."

"Someone has already gotten hurt, Ms. DelValle." Detective Pierce's baritone carried to her ear.

"With scissors?" she inquired, spinning them on her finger.

Felicia gave Dee a look and snatched the shears away.

"Is there some reason you're here today, Ms. DelValle?" The more shapely Detective Quinn joined her partner and looked at Dee.

"I missed Felicia's birthday party last night. Tully and I were going to take her out to celebrate." Dee nodded her head in Tully's direction.

"And you are?" Pierce inquired.

Tully never looked at him. In fact her gaze had never left

Gina Quinn's face once the detective had appeared. A grin spread across Tully's face as Quinn looked up from her notebook, waiting for an answer.

Tully's stare made Dee cast a more appraising look at the detective than she had last night. Glossy black hair, graying at the temples. Dark eyes—black or brown, Dee could not ascertain. Her olive complexion and prominent nose added to the Mediterranean look. Coupled with a strong, womanly body, she presented an attractive picture. Provided you didn't mind the exterior labeled "cop."

Dee and Felicia looked at each other as Tully's grin became intimate. "Tallulah Bouchart."

"Spell that for me, please, ma'am." Quinn's business-like reply did nothing to dampen Tully's smile. She moved to the detective's side, watching as she spelled each letter.

"And what is your relationship to the deceased?" Pierce's question still did not deflect Tully's stare.

"I was an acquaintance of Sheila's."

"Business or pleasure?" Quinn entry into the interview seemed to encourage Tully's smile. Before Tully could answer, Dee and Felicia moved out of earshot.

"Oh my God, is that girl playing out of her league." Felicia shook her head.

"Which one? If you mean Tully, she doesn't think she's in a league. She kinda figures she stands on her own."

"Well, I've got to say one thing for that hot little detective, she is playing it mighty cool."

"I know. I think she's about to set the world record for thaw time."

"Maybe she's taken. Notice her ring?"

Dee snorted. "That's never stopped Tully before. Or really even slowed her down."

"Honey, you'd think she'd have more sense than to take off after the woman who wants to send you up the river."

"Up the river?"

"Lock you up. String you up. Put on the cuffs and haul you away."

"I suspect Tully wouldn't be adverse to the cuffs, but she might draw the line at being strung up, although you never can tell."

Felicia didn't smile. "Girl, we've got to get serious. Those two are. I think they've talked to every single person here including the custodian and the mail carrier. They're more tenacious than a bloodhound after a rabbit that insulted his mother. We need to dig in."

"I'm not so sure about this. I understand Tully's concern, but investigating on our own might not be a good idea. Maybe the police will decide it wasn't murder, only a burglary gone bad. And maybe if I push on this, they'll lock me up for obstructing justice or practicing detecting without a license."

"And maybe they'll just lock you up for being the best suspect they've got on a well-publicized case." Felicia's eyes were stern. "Girlfriend, I have never known you to lie down and be walked on. What has gotten into you?"

Dee stared at the floor. She kicked at the worn berber carpet. "I don't know. I just don't seem to have been thinking too clearly lately."

Felicia reached out and brought Dee's chin up. Dark black eyes connected with green. "This isn't a gonad decision. This is a head one. And you have one of the hardest and levelest heads I know." Felicia paused and put her hand on Dee's shoulder. "So am I goin' to have to whoop your ass or are you goin' to shape up here and get with the program?"

Dee gave the carpet another kick. "I'll pass on the beating. Never been much into S/M." She ran her hand through her curls. "OK, Tonto, what do we do now?"

"Wait a minute. How did I get the sidekick assignment? You white folk are all alike. I swear I don't know when you are going to learn."

Dee held up her hand. "Hey, you want to be some kinky

white man who wears a mask all the time, the role is yours."

Felicia just snorted in response.

Dee glanced around at the people surrounding them. It was like a still-life picture that vibrated with energy. Most of the workers seemed rooted to their spots, but not one was relaxed. Remembering that all of these people knew each other, Dee asked Felicia, "What's been the reaction to Sheila's death around here?"

Felicia thought. "Shock. Surprise. Glee from some quarter."

"Glee?" Dee brightened at the prospect of other suspects. "I take it Sheila was not everyone's best friend."

"Tully wasn't alone in hating her, although hate's a strong word. Even people who didn't like Sheila respected her as a journalist. You know she had charisma. She was the star power for our local newscast. No one else came close. So it's more like jealousy. You know how it is in any business; those on the lower rungs want to climb."

"So which rung do you think I should start with?"

"Rachel!" Felicia's sudden yell caught Dee off-guard. "Come on over here, honey."

A lanky redhead strolled over to the two women. Her make-up was immaculate, but it couldn't hide the red of the rims of her eyes. She didn't smile in greeting, but, rather, nodded.

"Rachel O'Neil, I'd like you to meet my friend, Dee DelValle."

"Dee DelValle?" Rachel crossed her arms and cocked her head. "You were Sheila's latest little friend, weren't you?"

As Dee wondered how to respond, she studied Rachel's face. Aquamarine eyes surrounded by arched eyebrows set in the pale freckled skin so typical of natural redheads. Dee decided on a neutral question. "She mentioned me?"

"Oh, yes. She was quite impressed by your fervor over educational funding. She was researching a special report on the topic. You know, like the Pentagon spending two hundred dollars for a hammer."

Dee was taken aback. She remembered going over to

Sheila's one evening after a contentious Board of Education meeting she had attended as a faculty union representative. Once again the governor had signed an increase in school funding and once again the classrooms had no part in the trickle-down theory of educational finance. Special pork barrel programs of dubious worth had consumed the greater portion of the new monies.

Dee had come into Sheila's presence with a full head of indignant steam. She railed about the government and politics and the old boy network. After twenty-five minutes of Dee pontificating on the subject, Sheila excused herself. She returned barely wearing a peacock blue teddy which intensified the color of her eyes and set off her long legs as well as her other endowments.

The subject had been dropped.

In order to stop her brain from sending inappropriate messages to her body over the memory, Dee focused instead on her current mission. "I'm surprised that Sheila would share the idea for a special report, especially with a rival."

Rachel gave a rueful laugh. "I'm not sure you could really call us rivals. Besides, a piece which may or may not ever see the light of day is one thing, a scoop is another."

"But she did share that, and she spoke to you about me."

Rachel shrugged. "She'd mention what she was doing that night or on the weekend. You know how it is with office talk."

Dee wasn't sure she did. She glanced at the people now rushing back and forth. It seemed as if all of them knew their job with no need for interaction. Two men talking on cellular phones strode along, side by side. Every once in a while they spoke to each other. Dee figured it must be the newest method of having a conference. Somehow Channel 8 didn't seem like the kind of setting for the coffee pot chats Dee had seen on "Murphy Brown."

Dee tried a new tack. "It was really quite a jolt when I heard of her death. It was so bizarre to be waiting at a party, to be waiting for Felicia, and then hear the news." She shook her head.

"I know. I'll never forget it either." Rachel's voice caught. She swallowed before continuing. "I'd just come home from covering the five and six o'clock news desk. Sheila had taken the day off so I took her anchor slot. I was putting my purse down and kicking my shoes off when I heard it over the radio. I couldn't believe it. I still don't." Tears glistened in her already reddened and swollen eyes.

"What did you do?"

"I think I just froze. If Curtis hadn't come in just then, I don't know what I would have done."

"Curtis?"

"Curtis Lee. My husband."

A woman wearing blue jeans and a Grateful Dead tee shirt jogged up to Rachel. "A cop's been shot in Reseda. 7-11 hold up. Get on it." Without waiting for a reply, she jogged away, talking into the headphone that was inserted in one ear and wrapped over her hair.

Rachel followed, not stopping for goodbyes.

Felicia moved forward, crossing her arms and pursing her lips. "I'd never have guessed those two were that close."

"Sheila and Rachel? She really did seem upset."

The two friends stood in silent thought.

Dee asked. "Do you know her husband?"

"Curtis? Oh, sure. He's the director for the evening news. He just started about eight months ago. Little bit of a control freak, although that's not unusual for a director. Speaking of directors, here's the guy who should have gotten Curtis' job." Felicia gave another shout. "Hey, Fernando!"

A stocky, muscular man with deep brown skin and a worried face walked over and gave Felicia a hug. His cotton shirt was wrinkled and his salt and pepper hair darted from his head in all directions. He nodded at Dee when Felicia introduced them.

"Fernando is the assistant director on the evening news,"

she explained as she made the introductions.

"Assistant on the Titanic is more like it," Fernando muttered. "Have you seen the boss?"

Felicia shook her head. "I haven't seen Curtis at all this morning. How's he taking Sheila's death?"

"I haven't seen him yet either. I imagine he's out celebrating."

"Why's that?" Dee asked.

"His job's just gotten a whole lot easier. That is if he can control his wife better than he could Sheila."

"Are you saying Curtis and Sheila didn't get along?"

Fernando and Felicia looked at each other and gave a wry laugh. Fernando said, "That may be an understatement. Sheila could push all his buttons. Sometimes I thought he would go ballistic."

"What did they argue about?"

Fernando ran his hand over his face and through his disheveled hair. "All sorts of things. The amount of time Sheila got on camera. The investigative reports. The slant of the news."

Felicia chimed in. "I heard rumors they got into a shouting match the other day."

Fernando nodded. "Right after the newscast. Curtis was standing about five feet from me when Sheila came up really close to him and said something about telling the truth and he said something about it only being her version. Then she said something about what ends up in print is what's remembered. That's when I thought he was going to smack her one."

"When was all this?" Dee asked.

Fernando thought for a minute. "Wednesday? Thursday? Yeah, Thursday." He paused. "Geez, the day before she was killed."

Chapter 4

When the two friends returned to Felicia's work station, only Tully was there, twirling back and forth on the reclining swivel chair, a bemused look on her face.

"Don't tell me the mighty Casey has struck out?"

Tully grinned at Dee's taunt. "A temporary setback. We'll see what the future holds," she added as she held up a business card.

"Big deal. She gave me one, too, last night."

Tully's grin widened as she flipped the card over. "With her home phone number on the back?"

Felicia put her hands on her hips and a scold in her eye. "What did you tell her, girl? That you were some number one eyewitness or something?"

"Someday I'll write a book, and you poor women can pay good money to learn all my techniques. Until then, I give nothing away for free."

Dee sighed, "You know, I don't think Nancy Drew ever had this much trouble with George."

"Too true, sister." Felicia nodded in agreement. "But with that name, you do wonder what side of the road dear Ms. George wandered."

Crossing her arms, Dee gave Felicia and Tully her best disciplinarian stare. "Don't you start. We're supposed to be here investigating. Speaking of which, Felicia and I got off to a good start."

Dee and Felicia took turns filling Tully in on Rachel, Fernando, and Curtis.

"Is there anyone else whose feathers Ms. Shelbourne might have ruffled?" Tully asked Felicia.

Felicia thought for a moment. "Sheila was good at her job and she expected everyone else to be, too. That didn't set right with some. Guess Curtis was one of those. She also had a set to with one lighting tech, but he was fired about three months ago. She complained to the station manager when Curtis wouldn't do anything about the guy."

Dee was heartened at the apparent multitude of motives her co-workers had for killing Sheila. Jealousy, long-simmering anger, even career advantages! She began to think that Tully might have been right to push her to investigate. She just hoped the number of serious suspects did not end up numbering in the millions as Tully had foretold.

"Hey, sweetie!" A slender woman wearing jeans, cut-off sweatshirt, and a backwards baseball cap hailed Felicia from across the room. She walked towards them with a languid grace that seemed counter to the frenzied activity surrounding them.

Felicia again made introductions. "This sister is Marti Washington. She's the best camera tech this side of the Mississippi."

"I can only shoot what's in front of me. You're the one who makes the talking heads look beautiful." Adjusting her cap Marti said, "Now we'll all just have to get used to making a red-head look good rather than a blonde."

Felicia raised her eyebrows. "You sound sure that Rachel will get Sheila's job."

Marti pulled at her cap again. "I'm sure she will, at least in the short term. After all, who would they put in instead? Angela, the tap dancing weather girl, who can't tell the difference between smog and fog?" She chuckled softly at her own wit.

Dee studied the workers as they moved around the studio. She noticed that although the majority of the employees were males there were still a significant number of females. She asked Marti about that.

Marti explained that although there were many more women now than when she had started in the business, most were not behind the cameras. When asked, she identified the ones who were gay. "At least those are the ones I know about," she concluded.

"Do you know if Sheila dated any of them?" Dee asked.

Marti worked her jaw back and forth before answering. "Dated and dumped."

"All of them?" Dee asked incredulously.

"Most. Sheila treated monogamy like a four-letter word. She didn't seem to believe in it for herself," she paused, "or anyone else."

Felicia broke in with an abrupt change of subject. "Do you think the show's going to change now?"

Marti became more animated. "There'll be changes. You'll notice a difference in the look and feel of the show, the pacing and the timing as well as the coverage. The whole thing will be in different hands."

"But I thought Curtis Lee was in charge of the show, being the director and all," Dee said.

Marti raised one eyebrow, but did not reply. Instead she changed the subject. "By the way, do you know if Sheila ever finished that book of hers?"

"You mean that tell-all, trashy book she kept threatening to write?" Felicia asked.

"Oh, it wasn't a threat," Marti replied. "She was quite serious."

"What book is that and why did you stop me when I was asking about the women Sheila dated?" Dee demanded after Marti was pulled away by an even more harried looking Fernando.

People all around them were heading to the main section of the studio and the news desk set. The tumultuous sounds of voices and telephones had died down. The make-up area was all but deserted.

Felicia spoke in a low voice. "One of the women Sheila hooked up with was Annette, Marti's partner of nine years. The relationship ended after that and Annette left the show."

"But Marti didn't?"

Felicia shook her head. "No, but Sheila was shot from the wrong side for about a month after that. Drove Curtis crazy, but the camera crew just wouldn't cooperate."

Dee pondered the downside of angering the people who were responsible for presenting you to the world.

Felicia continued, "As for the book, it was supposed to be Sheila's autobiography."

"How come you didn't mention this book thing earlier?" demanded Tully.

Felicia put her hands on her hips and sighed. "First of all, it was just something Sheila's been talking about for a while. I never took it seriously. Secondly, just when was I supposed to have brought this up? I swear, you have the patience of a—"

"You three are at it again, I see. Looks like I arrived just in time." Jenny Felton's low voice floated over to them. A smile lit her angular face, as the pastels she habitually wore cast a soft glow across her pale skin. A tall, broad-shouldered woman with a prominent Adam's apple, she, nevertheless, always exuded total femininity. Jenny had filled out their foursome for the last three years, and so was used to the frequent good-natured squalls.

Felicia's frown was quickly replaced by a warm smile at the sight of Jenny. "You did indeed. As I was about to explain to our dynamic duo here, lunch may be the best plan of attack. With our good old police force making the rounds and the on-camera people occupied for the next hour or so, there's not much we can do here. If we go to lunch over at Dolly's Grill, I can give you the lowdown on all the gossip."

"Excuse me." Pierce, flanked by Quinn, ambled up to the

group. Both detectives scanned the women and then focused on Dee. "Ms. DelValle, will you be home later this afternoon? We have a few questions we'd like to ask you."

Chapter 5

Dee's feet hit an even rhythm as she completed mile two down Clark Street. She waited for an old pickup truck to pass, then made her customary crossing of the almost empty residential side street and headed, mercifully down hill, for the return two miles. This was the part of her run Dee enjoyed the most. As she jogged east, she'd watch the sun wash the clouds with the fuchsia and scarlet of the morning. But this early Monday the developing colors did not raise her spirits.

She knew she was in trouble.

Sunday afternoon Detectives Quinn and Pierce had been just as polite as before, but their questions were a lot more pointed. Exactly when was the last time she had visited Sheila at her condo? How had she gained access? Who had she talked to at the complex? What were the contents of Sheila's condo? Did anything there belong to her?

Dee finished her jog with a cool-down walk around her block. She unlocked the double deadbolts on her front door and entered the immaculate living room. She unclipped her pepper spray canister and headed for her bedroom. Instead of her usual post-run tranquil state of mind, her churning thoughts remained centered on yesterday's interview with the police.

She chewed over the answers she had given the whole time she showered and dressed for work. Guilt was growing in her, even though this time she had answered all their questions truthfully. At least, all the questions they had asked.

She still wasn't sure what had drawn the police back to her. Quinn and Pierce gave nothing away. But a weight in her belly told her they would be back again.

Her gloomy thoughts did not lighten at school. Even on a normal morning she dreaded reading lessons. Listening to children plod their way through a story with little comprehension and less joy did not make for an enthusiastic start to the day. Today the dreariness prompted her to call an early halt to the session and move on to science.

Dee congratulated herself on the decision. The students were enthusiastic about the electrical boards they were creating to illustrate the difference between parallel and serial circuits. Her mind was swept away from her own problems as she wandered from group to group helping them connect their handmade switches. She reveled in the joy of a successful lesson.

At least until Tom and Heidi, two of Dee's brighter students, decided that today was the day to create their own twist on the experiment. So while the rest of the class was engaged in causing lights to flash on and off and buzzers to sound, Tom and Heidi used their blunt-end scissors to cut open their D cell. Once the acid started to burn their fingers, Tom made matters worse by sticking his hand in his mouth. His subsequent howls attracted Dee's attention.

By the time the school nurse carted the two injured mad scientists away, Dee wanted to go home herself. That not being an option at ten in the morning, she instead took the surviving members of the class out for an early recess.

It was on the yard that the principal's summons reached her. Turning over control of her group to the yard duty teacher, Dee presented herself at the main office.

As soon as she entered the principal's office, she regretted ignoring her impulse to go home. Detectives Pierce and Quinn greeted her.

"Ms. DelValle, we'd like you to come down to the station with us." Gina Quinn's impassive face and hard eyes did not make it appear to be a social invitation.

One look told Dee that her status as a suspect had been elevated. For once she didn't relish being number one. She tried to put off the inevitable. "I'll be glad to come down after school. It's just that my plans aren't really good enough for a sub to follow and chances of finding a sub midday are slim. It might be hours before someone could take my class."

"I'm afraid this can't wait. I'm certain Mr. Johnstone," Quinn nodded at the principal, "will make sure your class is covered."

Hal Johnstone bobbed his round head at the detectives, never looking at Dee. "Yes, yes, indeed. I'll take care of it. No problem. No problem at all, officers." He reddened and tugged at his tie.

Dee considered helping Johnstone tug his tie quite a bit tighter. Recognizing the counter-productive nature of doing bodily harm to her principal in front of the detectives, Dee instead turned to him and said, "Hal, could you call Tully Bouchart? Her name is in the rolodex on my desk. Tell her what's happening."

The interrogation room's chair was slightly padded, the walls were blank but clean, and the temperature was warm without being stuffy. Dee should have been physically comfortable. She should have been overjoyed at not being in the classroom or in a negotiation session. She kept trying to tell herself these things, but somehow she wasn't buying them. Right now confronting the Board of Education seemed like Hawaii next to the Alaska-in-winter she was experiencing with Quinn and Pierce.

Dee ran her hand over her hidden tattoo and reflected that if they did a strip search of her and found the double-headed axe on her arm, they'd decide she was some crazed Amazon warrior and lock her up for good.

Rubbing her eyes, she sought to shift her thoughts, but they kept replaying the question she had hoped they wouldn't ask.

But Quinn had asked. Quinn. Sitting across the table with her shiny black hair and shiny dark eyes waiting for an answer. Dee didn't think even Tully would find Gina Quinn very appealing right now.

"Yes," Dee conceded, "I did go to Sheila's condominium Friday afternoon. I didn't see Sheila. But I did go there."

"Our witness said you went to Sheila's door."

"I went to the door. I put my hand on the knob because she said she'd leave the door unlocked for me. I stood there for maybe twenty seconds. Then I left."

"You never entered the condo?"

"No."

"You hadn't been in Sheila's home for three weeks?"

"That's right."

"Then how is it that your fingerprints are all over items in the condo—especially items in the living room?" Quinn added steel to her tone.

"She's a lousy housekeeper?"

Pierce, who had remained silent much of the interview, stood up from the corner chair. He leaned over the table towards Dee. "Look, you probably got there and she had this big seduction scene all ready for you—champagne, negligee, soft lights and music. Then something went wrong. Maybe she said something insulting, or maybe she threatened you if you didn't come across. Anyway, you got angry and panicked and picked up the statue and wham!" He slammed the table.

Pierce paused. "Then you decided to make it look like a robbery. You trashed the place. Threw over the bookshelves and smashed the computer. You tried to wipe off your fingerprints, but you forgot everything you touched." He shrugged his right shoulder.

Quinn picked up the theme, but with kindness in her voice. "You probably didn't mean to. I'm sure you had no intention of killing her when you went over. But things got out of hand."

Dee briefly considered how delighted she would be to hit

both Quinn and Pierce over the head right now. She pushed aside the impulse.

Pierce chimed in again. "And then you took it. Maybe you just wanted a memento. Or maybe your name was in it." This time he shrugged his left shoulder.

Dee entertained the thought that the alternating shoulder shrug might be a tai chi form of police calisthenics. Then curiosity overtook her wandering train of thought. "I'll bite. What did I take to remember Sheila by?"

Pierce looked at Quinn who nodded. "You took her day planner."

"Her day planner?" Dee snorted. "How romantic. I just killed my ex-lover and looking around her place I find her date book and decide to take it with me for old time's sake? Do you two really get paid for inventing these scenarios?"

"We can get a search warrant for your house."

"If you could get one, you would have gotten one already. Since you haven't, it shows me you know that all this is flimsy nonsense."

Gina Quinn smiled without humor. "We can keep you for questioning while we build an even better case."

The veiled threat caught Dee's full attention. She began to wonder just how deep the hole was that she had dug for herself. "I want to call a lawyer."

"We asked you that at the beginning," Pierce said, with a glance at the running tape recorder. "You said you didn't want one."

"I changed my mind."

Quinn nodded to Pierce, who left the room. "There's an attorney outside. Alex has gone to get her."

Dee's eyebrows rose. "You just have lawyers sitting around outside the police station waiting to be needed?"

Gina Quinn leaned back in her chair, not meeting Dee's look. "Some friends of yours contacted this one. But since you didn't want one…"

"…you didn't tell me one was there, right?" Dee finished Quinn's thought.

Quinn stared at the beige wall.

"Which friends called this attorney?"

"Evelyn Taylor and Tully Bouchart."

Dee noted Quinn's use of Tully's nickname, but that item of interest was overwhelmed by the knowledge of Evie's involvement in the proceedings.

Marsha Brown had lawyer written all over her. She strode into the room and threw the detectives out. "Have you answered any questions?" She drilled Dee with her look.

"Well, sure."

"No more. Not unless they charge you with something. And then only with me present. Is that clear?"

Dee could tell Marsha's drill sergeant attitude would allow no resistance. She relaxed for the first time in days.

"What do you mean you were there?" Tully's usual slow drawl edged toward anger.

Tully and Dee sat at Dee's kitchen table. Although the chair had more padding and the table was oak, to Dee the scene was becoming reminiscent of the interrogation room. When Tully first picked her up outside police headquarters, Dee had been thrilled to see her. Now she wished she had called a cab.

Dee looked at the oak and traced the wood grain pattern with her fingers. "Sheila left me a message Thursday evening saying she had some news and wanted to tell me about it. But it was a surprise and could I please come over Friday after work. She said she needed my help. She was taking the night off and she'd be home and she'd leave the door unlocked for me."

Freed of her self-imposed silence, Dee could feel the story bursting from her mouth. She looked up at Tully. "I drove over after school. I got there around five. The whole time one part of my brain was shouting at me, but it wasn't until I put my hand on her doorknob that I finally understood what the voice was saying."

Dee stood and grabbed the pitcher of iced tea off the tiled kitchen counter. She waited until she had refilled both their glasses before continuing her saga. "I realized that opening her door would be the stupidest thing I could do. It would even out-rank my original stupidity in getting involved with her. So I left. I felt guilty, embarrassed, and miserable. Kind of like now." She swallowed her drink with difficulty.

Tully pushed with her feet and rocked her chair on its two back legs. She sat that way for several minutes, rocking and staring out the window at Dee's back yard. She dropped the front legs gently and turned to look at Dee. "Is there anything else you haven't told me?" The gentle Texan drawl was back.

Dee shook her head.

"Nothing you're holding back because I haven't asked the right question?"

This time Dee blushed, but she still shook her head no.

Tully nodded. "Well, you know, this all might turn out to be a good thing. A very, very good thing."

Chapter 6

Ignoring Dee's disbelieving stare, Tully unfolded her long body and reached for the grocery list pad Dee had hanging on the side of the refrigerator. She also grabbed a pencil from a drawer before settling herself again. Tully tapped the pencil on the paper. "We're in the driver's seat. You're a direct witness. You probably know things that the police don't. We'll be ahead of the game."

"That's presuming I know something. Which I don't."

"Sure you do. It's like the purloined letter. It's sitting in front of you, but you don't see it because it blends in with its surroundings." She drew a line down the middle of the page. "What did you see when you pulled up to Sheila's building?"

Dee closed her eyes. "I parked almost in front of her condo complex. There was a man with a black briefcase walking down the street. I remember because he almost ran into me as I was getting out of my car."

"Anybody you know?"

"No. Just a guy. Funny thing was he was wearing a hat. You know, like one of those felt hats guys wore in the forties?" She glanced at Tully. "You just don't see guys wearing dress hats anymore."

"Fashion notes aside, what else did you see?"

"There were two people outside the building. An older, white haired man and a very tall, slender woman. I think the woman was a tenant in the building. She looked familiar."

"Was she there when you left?"

"No."

"Any other people?"

"Not outside. At least not on that side of the street."

Tully tapped her teeth with the pencil. "How did you get in?"

"One woman was letting herself into the front gate. She had four or five bags from Neiman Marcus and was trying to juggle them and unlock the bolt at the same time. I guess she recognized me from previous visits because she let me help her with the packages and with opening the gate."

"Did she see you go to Sheila's door?"

Dee thought. "I'm not sure. We rode up together on the elevator and we got off on the same floor, but she went left while I went right down the hall."

"Did you see anyone else in the hallway?"

Dee shook her head.

"OK, partner," Tully said, "let's back up. Did you see any cars when you first arrived?"

Dee closed her eyes and got images of driving the streets of the Wilshire District, turning on a narrow side street, parking at the curb. "There were two cars close together and then one a ways in front of me. That left a big space for me and I was grateful since parallel parking is not my best driving skill."

"Terrific." Tully added to the list on the paper. "Now, what kind of cars were they?"

"God, Tully. You know me and cars. I can't tell a Volkswagen from an Oldsmobile."

"Considering how they're making them nowadays, that's not a surprise." Tully continued her drum solo, pencil on pad. "All right, let's try this. You know my Jeep. Sheila drove a Mercedes, right? And Felicia has a Mazda RX and Jenny's car is a Honda Civic. Did any of them look like any of those?"

"None of them were convertibles like Sheila's. And I don't recall seeing a little metal peace sign on the front of the cars."

"I'm sure the Mercedes Corporation would love your

description of their logo."

Dee ignored the interruption. "No flashy cars. Wait, one was a BMW. Black. It was right behind me. The other two..." She shook her head in frustration.

"Were all three cars still there when you came out?"

Dee rubbed her face and ran her hands over her hair. "The BMW and the one behind that were gone. There was a different car in front of mine. It was between my car and the car ahead." She waved her finger in the air. "That one was a Honda! A forest green Honda! I remember the funny upside-down goal-post H on the back. I looked because it had a gay pride license plate holder. I always look when I see one of those."

Tully noted the information and returned to rocking. "I just thought of something. You said you stood at Sheila's door for a few minutes before you turned around and left, right?"

Dee, still wrapped up in the excitement of having identified a car, took a moment to follow Tully's leap. "Yes. I stood there like a mime with my hand on the door and my brain on freeze."

"Did you hear anything from the condo?"

"I don't think so."

"Dee, good buddy, you're all we have. Think hard. Were there any sounds? TV? Talking? Yelling? Pounding?"

Dee closed her eyes again and tried to relive those few moments. "I had the feeling she was in there and it wasn't just that I expected her to be. Now what made me think that?" She slipped into silence. Her eyes flew open. "I heard her voice! You know how distinctive her voice was. She was talking. At the time I thought she must be on the phone because why would there be someone with her if she was expecting me, but—"

Tully broke in. "But, what if she were talking to the murderer?"

Chapter 7

"I hate funerals."

Dee's petulance was ignored by Tully as she navigated the tree-shaded curves of Sunset Boulevard. The Jeep bounced over the rise and fall of the windy road which led from the cemetery to the home of Mr. and Mrs. Shelbourne.

"Funerals may not be great, but wakes are the perfect place to pick up clues. Everyone's relieved the funeral's over and they're well lubricated with drink. What better time to interrogate a few prime suspects? And her folks will be off-guard. They might give us some leads."

"Off-guard? Grief-stricken, bereaved, hysterical even." Dee was tempted to throw up her hands, but she didn't want to lose her grip on the dashboard. "And how do we go about getting them to spill the beans? I haven't been the most successful interrogator."

"Good grief. You're a teacher. You've told me that all you have to do is pretend to already know the truth. The guilty can't wait to confess."

"That sometimes works with kids. I'm not sure adults operate with the same mentality. Plus, what makes you think they have some guilty secret ready to pop forth?"

"We all have guilty secrets," Tully said, as she parallel parked along a stretch of the Pacific Palisades. "That's what makes life interesting."

As they alighted from the Jeep, both women scanned the

cars parked along the street. No fewer than four black BMW's graced the block, but no Hondas, with or without rainbow license frames.

Tully drew out the list and noted the license plates. She grinned at Dee. "Going to be doggone interesting trying to find out what kind of car everyone drives."

They strolled up the Shelbourne's walkway. The cool ocean breeze fought with the warm sunshine for dominance. Bright pansies and miniature geraniums bordered the cement path which led to double oak doors. Ornate leaded-glass windows almost covered the top third of both doors.

Tully winked at Dee. "Five will get you ten that Lurch opens the door."

Although not massive nor bald, the ashen man who answered their knock did bear some resemblance to the infamous Addams Family butler. And he was just about as talkative. After a mute moment of staring, he nodded at them and said, "Family's in there." The nod of his head directed them through an arch shaped doorway into the sitting room.

In another house it may have been the family room, but the unrelenting whiteness of carpeting and wooden furniture gave it all the homey welcome of an airport departure gate. Even the fireplace was decked with white marble. Only flowers brought life to the room. Multitudinous bouquets, arrangements, and funeral sprays occupied every table.

Dee recognized Sheila's mother and father from a picture in Sheila's condo. Mrs. Shelbourne sat leaning forward on a love seat while her husband stood beside her. Even from a distance, it was obvious that Sheila had inherited her green eyes from her mother. Her blonde hair was, no doubt, a tribute to hairdressing considering both parents displayed deep brown waves. However, in Mr. Shelbourne's case, time had clear cut part of his forest of brown.

Tully broke into Dee's scrutiny. "Ma and Pa?" she asked with a nod towards the Shelbournes.

"The same."

"Anyone else you recognize?"

Dee scanned the scene. About twenty people filled the space, some with faces familiar from local TV.

"That's Rachel O'Neil. You know, the roving reporter, the one I talked with." Dee pointed her chin towards the fireplace.

Rachel stood with her hands in the slash pockets of her camel-colored slacks listening to a tall, slender man. She stared at him as he flung his arms to punctuate his comments. Her smooth red pageboy caught the light each time she moved her head.

"I know who she is," Tully said. "Who's the string bean next to her?"

"I never met him, but I think that must be her husband, Curtis Lee, the news director. Felicia likes him, but he's not someone Sheila had much respect for."

"Why no respect?"

"I'm not sure. It was something Sheila mentioned about his lack of ability or background or something. I had the feeling he bought his way into his position and you know Sheila, if there was one thing she couldn't stand it was being around incompetent people."

"I heard she was a bit of a perfectionist."

"The worst."

"In bed as well as out?" Tully's eyebrows danced.

Dee rolled her eyes and turned away. She touched Tully's arm. "Hey, the cavalry has arrived." They watched Felicia and Jenny walk together into the whitewashed room.

"Was this another chauffeuring assignment you gave Jenny?"

"Nope. Maybe Felicia's southern charms are finally making some inroads." Tully nudged Dee in the ribs. "You know, if Felicia hadn't been Sheila's makeup artist on the show, you'd never have met that twit."

Dee hushed her. "She wasn't a twit. Have some respect.

Besides, if we go into the 'if only' realm then, if only my last name and Felicia's hadn't been close together in the alphabet, we never would have been seated together in school. And if only she hadn't met you while you were doing that ad job for the station, then I never would have met you. And if only I hadn't met you I wouldn't be in this God-awful living room right now pondering the intricacies of the universe."

"That's true. You'd probably be in jail."

Silenced, Dee watched as Felicia reached out and held Mrs. Shelbourne's hands. They exchanged some words, which caused Mrs. Shelbourne to burst into tears and Mr. Shelbourne to squeeze her shoulder. Felicia stepped back from the scene just as Jenny touched her on the arm and nodded in Dee and Tully's direction.

Jenny greeted Tully with a kiss as Felicia wrapped her long, café au lait arms around Dee. "Oh, girlfriend, I'm so sorry I had to miss the funeral. Somebody had to work. Although looking around here, you'd never know there was anyone back at the station."

Jenny looked down at her large feet, then enveloped Dee in an embrace. "I still can't believe the police think you had anything to do with this."

"Speaking of the police, our favorite detectives were at the funeral."

Jenny's eyes grew large. "Were they watching you?"

Dee shook her head. "But I do know someone who was watching them. Or at least one very shapely member of the duo."

Three pair of eyes turned to Tully. Plastering an innocent look on her face she smiled and said, "No harm in looking."

Felicia snorted. "Your looks are like a normal person's leers. Any thawing of the ice maiden?"

"Not yet."

Jenny's alto broke in. "God, woman. Can't you keep your mind out of bed and on the job? It's your best buddy's life we're talking about here."

"It just so happens, we are just about to check out the queen and king on the couch. What are you two going to do?"

Felicia jerked her head to the left. "I thought we'd check with the people who aren't with the news team. See who they are and what their ties might be."

Tully nodded. "Make sure you check on their taste in automobiles at the same time."

After agreeing to meet up later and compare notes, Dee and Tully headed towards Sheila's parents.

Dee whispered to Tully as she neared the Shelbournes. "Any suggestions?"

"Play it by ear."

Sighing, Dee extended her hand to Mrs. Shelbourne. "I'm Diega DelValle and this is my friend, Tully Bouchart. Your daughter and I, uh, saw each other, socially. And I just wanted to tell you how sorry I was to hear of her passing."

"That is so kind of you. I don't know all of Sheila's friends. I hadn't even met all of her business associates until now." A brief spasm crossed her face.

Moved by her pain, Dee perched on the edge of the couch beside her and took her hands as Tully slipped away. She tried to find some words of comfort, but since Sheila had only mentioned her parents once, and not in the best terms, Dee felt at a loss. She decided a slight whitewashing of the truth was the only kindness. "I want you to know that Sheila was a warm and loving woman as well as a talented news reporter. A lot of that credit has to go to you."

Mrs. Shelbourne's cat's eyes glistened with tears. "You know she was a three-time champion in the Junior Miss Pageant? How she loved dressing up and having me fix her hair. Isn't that right, Henry?"

The silent Mr. Shelbourne nodded.

"She liked to compete, didn't she?" Dee ventured.

"Oh, Lord, yes. Even as a little girl she loved to go out and do her best. Henry, honey, do you remember when they were giving out that prize in San Diego—you know—that broadcast thing?"

"The Balboa Trophy," Mr. Shelbourne said in a tenor voice that matched his slender body.

"That's it. Well it went to the best news journalist and Sheila knew she was up against some little hick from Ohio or somewhere and she knew she needed something really good to win. She used her contacts in the police department. They notified her as soon as they got the first call on this bank robbery. She was there even before her station had sent a team! She filed her story using her cellular phone, beat every newscast in the area, and won that prize hands down. That's Sheila. She was always determined to be the best and she's... The light faded from Mrs. Shelbourne's eyes. "She's—"

A fresh swelling of tears brought Henry to his wife's side. Dee slid over the brocade seat of the couch to allow him to take her place. As she eased away she heard him say, "Now, Mandy, get a grip. Don't make a scene."

Feeling worse instead of better informed, Dee's eyes searched for Tully. Instead she spotted Rachel at the buffet table, no husband in sight. Deciding that there might be additional information to be gained from the newswoman, she joined her at the table.

"Hi."

Dee's greeting caused Rachel to jump. A look of confusion transformed to one of recognition. "Dee, right? I saw you at the funeral."

Conversation about the ceremony flowed easily as they picked over the small sandwiches and fruit and vegetable plates. Dee turned the talk to work.

"Who'll take Sheila's place, do you suppose?" Dee wondered if her voice sounded innocent enough. It both pleased and frightened her to think she was getting the hang of the duplicity necessary for investigative success.

Rachel twitched her upper lip. "They'll probably bring in someone from the outside. Nightly anchor is a plum spot. You can leap to bigger markets from there." She plucked a sliver of red bell pepper and slid it into the basil sour cream dip before placing it in her mouth.

"I'd have thought you'd be the logical successor. You've got the name recognition, the background, the history with the network," Dee paused, then added, "not to mention the good looks."

Eyes narrowing, Rachel stared. "Whatever you're selling, I'm not buying."

"What do you mean?"

"Look, I know you and Sheila were not just friends. So, if you're some TV anchor groupie, forget it. I'm a happily married woman." This time Rachel jabbed the bell pepper into the dip.

Flustered, Dee decided to try to return to her main line of inquiry. "I wasn't trying to pick you up. Really." She raised her left hand, placed her right on her heart, and gave her most sincere smile. "I was just surprised that you weren't automatically named to the position."

Rachel looked Dee in the eyes, as if weighing a decision. "Politics," came the eventual reply. "Plus I'm up for a national reporting job. Network managers know I'm being considered so they don't want to put me in the slot and then be embarrassed by my leaving in a month."

"I'd think they'd offer you the job to make sure you'd stay."

Rachel snorted. "You've got to be kidding. No one in her right mind would give up a national spot for a local news anchor position—no matter how big the market." With that she wandered off leaving Dee to stare at the buffet.

"Vultures. All of them." Curtis Lee's look swept the whole of the crowd before coming to rest on Dee. "I suppose you're one, too." He threw the rest of his drink down his throat.

Guessing she was dealing with one who was none too sober, Dee asked, "Vultures?"

"Vultures," Curtis affirmed as clinked his glass down on a nearby side table. "Picking over the dead. Sometimes when they're still alive."

"Sheila's job?" Dee ventured, unconsciously copying his staccato delivery.

"Sheila's. Rachel's. Mine. Probably even yours." His brown eyes focused on her. "Who the hell are you anyway?"

"Diega DelValle. A friend of Felicia's."

"Diega? Hell of a name. Familiar though. San Diega?"

"Nobody's put me up for sainthood that I know about." Debating which tack to take with this obviously inebriated man, Dee studied Curtis' face. She thought his elongated head looked as though someone had grabbed his chin and forehead at birth, pulling in opposite directions. It was not, she decided, an attractive look, but it was a distinctive one. Knowing she had, many times, rued her own heart-shaped face, she tried not to pass judgment on Curtis'. Steering the subject to more fertile grounds, she asked, "What's all the competition about?"

Curtis waved his hand. "TV-Q. Ratings. Not experience. Not ability."

Dee attempted a translation. "The network managers don't think you have the name recognition to take Sheila's place?"

Curtis looked at her with disdain. He flagged a passing waiter and chugged half a glass of wine before resuming. "Not me. Rachel. Give her half a chance and she'll zoom the numbers."

"I thought Rachel didn't want the job."

"Not want it? L.A. prime time nightly? Biggest market outside New York? She'd kill for it."

Chapter 8

Walking down the Shelbourne's garden path, Dee asked Tully, "What happened to Felicia and Jenny?"

"Jenny got called back to the hospital. Evidently some celebrity was just admitted and the powers that be wanted an immediate press release. You know how it goes when you're the PR front man."

"Or woman." Jenny had become a familiar face on local TV. In fact, Dee remembered that Sheila once interview Jenny about a rock star who overdosed. Dee stopped to admire the red geraniums. "Maybe I should put some of these along the front walk of my place. Jazz it up a bit."

Tully raised an eyebrow. "You? Ms. Brown Thumb?"

Ignoring her friend's reaction, Dee continued, "Did they find out anything before they left?"

"Yep. Every single production hand they talked with was either working that night or in the presence of at least three other people, including Fernando, the assistant director and Marti, the wronged camera woman. And nobody was bubbling forth with any brilliant observations or motives."

"Then this was a waste of time," Dee said as she climbed into the passenger's side of the Jeep.

"Not at all, Miss Marple," Tully replied with a grin as she hopped into the driver's seat. "I know who owns three of the Beemers and just wait till you hear who Lurch is."

"Lurch? The guy at the front door?"

"The one and only. His name is Steve Montgomery and he's the former Mr. Sheila Shelbourne."

Dee turned her stunned face towards Tully. "Sheila was married? To a man?"

"It's been known to be allowed among some primitive tribal peoples."

"When was this?"

"I got the scoop from a woman named Aurora who's the lighting tech. Seems she worked the same San Diego news show Sheila did. And Sheila had just divorced Mr. Steve, who was none too keen about the break-up. Even came to the studio once to threaten her. Sheila called the police on him."

"Holy moly!" Dee felt a glow of excitement. "But how does this Aurora person know all this?"

"She happened to be Sheila's hot tamale at the time and Steve Montgomery's threat included bodily harm to them both."

"Has she told the police this yet?"

"Yep. But she said they didn't seem much interested since it all happened seven years ago."

"I wonder if they even bothered to check out Mr. Montgomery's whereabouts on Friday night."

"Don't know. But I do know that one of those black beauties of a BMW belongs to him."

Dee eyes widened even more. "That moves him up the suspect list, wouldn't you agree? Who else is the proud owner of those fine automobiles?"

"Curtis Lee for one and Mr. Shelbourne for another. Although I'm not sure that his was one of the ones parked in the street. Makes for interesting conjectures doesn't it?"

Dee gripped the side handle as Tully threw the Jeep around a curve. "It would if I could give either of those guys a half-way decent motive. Maybe Sheila was threatening to cut off her support to her parents. Maybe Curtis wanted to clear the way to the anchor position for his wife. Maybe it was an FBI conspiracy."

"No more 'X-Files' for you." Tully stared at the road. "Do you think the good Detective Quinn might be interested in some of these more rational tidbits?"

Dee shook her head. "You'll use any excuse to contact her, won't you?"

Tully remained silent as she whipped the Jeep through the turn from Sunset to the even curvier Benedict Canyon Road which led through the hills separating the West Side from the San Fernando Valley. Two-story homes with brick and stone facades faced the street from discreet distances behind their gated fences and perfectly trimmed lawns.

After one of the more daring curves, Tully asked, "So you really got nothing from anyone there?"

"Just the distinct impression that Rachel and Sheila were probably more than just good friends."

"Why am I not surprised?" Tully sniffed. "Actually, some guys would be pretty angry over that. Does Rachel's hubby know?"

"Not that I could tell. He seemed more concerned with her taking over the anchor spot than anything else. It made me wonder if the two of them ever talk to each other."

"What do you mean?"

"Well, Rachel says she wants the national spot and Curtis says she wants the local anchor position. Do you think it could be a negotiating ploy?"

"If you were the network brass, maybe. Buy why would they be putting on an act with you?"

"Hell, if I knew why anyone was doing anything I'd be a whole lot happier."

"Well," Tully said, as she pulled up in front of Dee's suburban tract home, "Jenny and Felicia and I are helping you because we love you. Does that make you happy?"

"I'm glad someone is pure and clean."

Dee paused outside her front door. She turned and looked at her trim green lawn and the symmetrical green rounded bushes which grew against her house. Dissatisfied with all she surveyed, she unbolted the door.

The message light on her answering machine was blinking when she entered the house. She walked past it and pulled a Pacifico beer from the refrigerator. Only after downing half the bottle did she poke a finger at the playback button.

"Dee? It's Evie. Call me when you get a chance."

Dee let the machine click. She walked into her bedroom, hung up her funeral finery, and changed into jeans and a tee shirt. Pausing at the mirror, she regarded her image. She placed the beer bottle on the night stand long enough to roll up her sleeves and expose the battle axe tattooed on her upper arm. Then she grabbed money and her keys and headed for the nursery.

Four hours later she wiped the stinging sweat from her forehead and neck and regarded her home. Six of the eight bushes were stuffed in the green recycling barrel in the driveway. In their place was a staggered front row of scarlet verbena, salmon Sweet William, and orchid vincas. Behind those stood lavender and yellow snapdragons, purple salvia, and orange marigolds. Dee had been disappointed to learn that she was too late to get bare root roses, but she made a vow to include those next year.

"About time you put in some color."

Dee whirled. Her heartbeat slowed when she realized it was just her next-door neighbor replete in her straw gardening hat. "Hi, Mrs. Holmes. Didn't know you were out here."

"Amy. I've told you to call me Amy. 'Mrs. Holmes' makes me feel older that I am. And that's old enough." She picked up her cane and pointed it at Dee. "You looked like you were going jump on the roof when I called to you. Why are you such a nervous Nellie today?"

"Guess I was just too absorbed in the planting."

Amy Holmes grunted and shifted her weight onto her cane. "Those salvia and verbena won't last much longer. And that Sweet William will spread all over. Why didn't you put in roses?"

Amy Holmes' entire front garden was filled with roses.

"I didn't want to compete with you."

Amy gave another snort. "You couldn't if you tried." She limped back into her house.

After a shower and the opening of her second beer, Dee picked up the telephone and dialed. "Evie? Hi. I got your message."

"I've been worried about you." Evie's voice held warmth as well as concern.

"I've been worried about me, too. But things seem to have calmed down. Thanks for giving Tully the lawyer's name."

"No problem. I guess Marsha must have been of help since you're not in jail."

"Mainly she told me to shut up. I always feel guilty if someone asks me a question and I don't answer it, like I'm really guilty. And some of their questions didn't seem so bad, but she didn't want me to say anything and you know the worst part?" Dee continued without pause. "Marsha didn't even want to know whether or not I killed Sheila. She actually told me she preferred not to know. O.J. should have grabbed her for his team."

"When you jabber like this, it makes me suspect there's something going on."

Dee could picture Evie peering through her large round glasses. It sometimes seemed as if those glasses gave her x-ray vision. "Yeah, well, I wanted to apologize." Silence hung like a cloud heavy with rain. "I mean, I never really told you I was sorry for everything that happened."

"You mean your cheating or your lying? Or was there something else that I still don't know about? And if there is, I don't want to hear it."

Dee let the silence build again as she glanced out the living room window. Her quiet residential street was typically the playground for the neighborhood children. She reflected that school must be out for the day since the usual ball game was under way. She blew across the narrow neck of the beer bottle creating a low, mournful note. She took another sip then said, "Maybe this isn't the best time to talk about what happened."

"Especially not if you're drinking in the middle of the day."

"Beer doesn't count as drinking. Especially if you've been questioned by the police, almost thrown in jail, and scrutinized during the funeral of the woman you were supposed to have beaten to death." Dee paused to take a breath. "Whiskey. Now there's drinking. Unfortunately, I hate the taste." With that, she tilted her head back and drained the bottle.

Evie's sigh echoed through the twenty miles of phone lines that separated them. "While you are still sober enough to comprehend this, I want you to know that two charming police detectives did, indeed, come to visit me. What I don't understand is why they were asking me about your sports activities."

"Sports? What kind of sports?"

"They were vague. I told them we played tennis and softball together."

"Did they ask anything else?"

"They asked if you batted right or left handed." Evie answered after a moment's thought. "I told them what a hopeless southpaw you are. Remember the time you sprained your left wrist and couldn't move your hand? I thought you were going to be reduced to eating off your plate because you certainly weren't getting too far using you right hand."

Dee recalled the frustration of that softball injury and the reaction of Evie who not only fed and bathed her but dressed her as well with great patience and kindness. Warmth spread across her chest. "You were terrific with me. Especially considering I was never a model patient."

"You weren't as bad as all that." Silence again descended. Then Evie cleared her throat. "So, you don't know what the sports deal was about?"

Dee turned to again look out her front window while she considered the question. A small, snub-nosed girl connected with the pitch sending the ball bouncing off the brown Buick two doors down. Dee swore. "Oh my God."

"What?"

"I wonder which side of Sheila's head got whacked."

Chapter 9

"Sheila Shelbourne? You were dating the Sheila Shelbourne? And you never told me?" Jim Tolkien's double chin would have registered 6.5 on the Richter Scale had it impacted anything other than his chest.

Dee just shook her head at the other half of her teaching team and surveyed her desk with dismay.

Dee had arrived at her classroom at seven AM, prepared for complete chaos. Much to her relief it appeared that Principal Johnstone had not only found a real substitute teacher to take her class on Monday, but, miracle of miracles, the same person had returned Tuesday. No matter the quality of the sub, though, it always took two days of work to catch up with one day's absence. At that rate, Dee figured she might be even by the end of June.

"Murder." Jim shook his head. "Well that beats Edna Fisher's suggestion that they were finally taking you away for your disgraceful lifestyle."

"Ah, dear Edna." Dee had arrived at her first faculty Christmas party with a date. To Edna's dismay, Dee's date was a woman. Edna Fisher had choked on her glass of port and given Dee the evil eye ever since. "I bet she was titillated at the thought of sodomy charges."

"Too bad for her the detectives had an unmarked car. She would have loved to see you being dragged away with the red lights flashing."

"Considering Edna thinks teaching would be a great job if it weren't for the children, I can think of worse people to hate me."

Wading through the forms, messages, notes, and papers piled upon her desk, Dee said a prayer for all the trees killed daily by the Glendale Unified School District.

Jim perched one hip on the only clear corner of her desk. He taught down the hall from Dee and they were in the habit of dropping in on each other in the mornings, especially since this last year when Jim had talked Dee into joining the union's negotiation team.

His pudgy frame and sleepy eyes hid an intellect that could dissect and construct arguments with an acuity that would be the envy of most trial lawyers. The only outward sign of his inner workings was his right foot. The faster it bounced, the harder he was thinking. His foot was flying at the moment. "Dug down far enough to get to my memo about the team meeting on Thursday?"

"I'm sure I'll find it by Friday."

Jim twirled a pen he found under a stack of While You Were Out memos. "Our beloved principal has made an informal request to the union regarding you."

"Now what is spineless Hal up to?"

"He wants to know if he can put you on administrative leave while you're under investigation. He thinks the suspicion of guilt might have a disruptive effect on your classroom."

"That wart-covered toad." Dee kicked back her chair and regarded Jim. "Hal isn't shrewd enough to even think of the possibility. Who do you think is pressuring him?"

"Besides Edna? Probably some of our Board of Ed members. Nothing they'd like better than a little scandal to shake our ranks."

Dee chewed her lower lip. "How would they know anything? Unless that brown-nosed little slime bag in the front office called and told them." She ran her hand through her curls. "I'm not going to let some weak-kneed administrator run me out of my own classroom. It's bad enough the police have it out for me, I'm not going to be run roughshod by some two-bit, know-nothing, lily-livered..." Noticing Jim's silence, Dee added, "Feel free to join me anytime."

Jim tapped the pen on his knee but didn't respond.

Dee began to feel empathy for those who had not survived the sinking of the Titanic. "The union wants me out, too, doesn't it?"

Jim seemed fascinated by the bouncing pen. "The union executive board doesn't want you out. Who else would be fool enough to volunteer as editor of the newsletter? Still, murder." The pen bounced faster. "Now I understand why our illustrious president was upset. George doesn't do well with upsets."

"George wants me gone?"

Dee knew the president of the union, George Carvel, well, and liked him not at all. Carvel talked a great game when campaigning, but he hated confrontations. He left those to the negotiating team. She swiveled her chair while reviewing her possibilities. "Who else?"

"Nobody else knows. Nothing official."

"They can't make me take a leave if I haven't been legally charged with anything, can they?"

Jim shook his head as he gazed out the Venetian blinds of the schoolroom's windows. The sun was already casting slats of light and dark on the linoleum floor. He stood, still not facing Dee. "There's bound to be more gossip, more whispers. Parents will hear. Kids will talk." Jim shrugged his shoulders and faced his teaching partner. "Why couldn't you stick to unknown women for your affairs? You'd save yourself a lot of trouble."

Dee looked away from his face and stared at the acoustical tiles of the ceiling. "It's a little late for that thought, Jim, but I'll keep it in mind for next time."

Jim put his hand on Dee's shoulder. "I really don't want to go into those final few negotiation sessions without you. You know the Board will eat the team alive without your numbers to back us up. If you took some time off now, do you think you could clear this all up in a week or so?"

"Me clear it up? I thought that was the job of the police."

"Seems to me that if the police are busy questioning you, they have their heads stuck where the sun don't shine." He squeezed her shoulder and started to walk out the door. "If it were me, I wouldn't hold my breath waiting for them to solve this."

Dee hung her school clothes and dug out a fresh pair of jeans and an old tee shirt. As she dressed she tried to decide what to do.

Being home in the middle of the day during a weekday gave Dee mutinous thoughts of retirement at age thirty-four. She spent a moment envying Tully and her substantial trust fund. Although Tully refused to tap its resources, it supplied her with the financial security to work as she saw fit in a freelance photography job whose paychecks were unreliable.

The thought of unknown and uneven income gave Dee a nervous tick. As did the thoughts of growing up with an absent father whose idea of support was purely financial. Dee's envy of Tully's life, as usual, passed as soon as she envisioned giving up her own exuberant and large family for Tully's lonely upbringing.

Dee wandered into her workroom. The rainbow of colors from her Latin American weavings welcomed her. Sunlight flowing through the sheer curtains warmed the room. She relaxed into her oversized leather executive chair and let the peace of her sanctuary fill her.

This was the only room in her house she had designed herself. Nancy Yegarian and another friend were budding interior decorators and had offered to choose the furnishings for her home as a housewarming present. Having little interest in such matters, Dee had given them free reign in the rest of the house, but had barred them from her workroom.

Dee smiled as she scanned the hundreds of books lining the low shelves around the room. For a moment she considered digging into her art closet and working out her aggressions on some clay, but the prospect seemed far too energetic. Instead she sank lower into the soft leather and reflected on the last few days.

The reality that the police were zeroing in on her as the number one suspect made her long for a candy bar. Somehow the thought of jail didn't seem so bad if it was covered in chocolate. Chocolate. One of the several passions she and Sheila had shared.

Dee remembered their first evening together. Sheila had unearthed an ancient fondue pot. They melted chocolate and dipped bananas and hot-house strawberries in it. Dee had glimpsed a Sheila very different from the posed, confident, and commanding woman who controlled the news anchor desk. Here was a woman who laughed as chocolate ran down her chin and who reached over to lick the chocolate off Dee's fingers.

Dee soon classified Sheila as an odd combination of romantic hedonist and driven career woman. Sheila would send Dee flowers the colors of the sunset they had seen the night before and then forget their dinner date the next day because a story broke or she was following a lead.

After the first month, there were fewer flowers and more broken dates. Bowing to the inevitable, Dee bid Sheila goodbye. Little did Dee realize that Evie had already caught on and shortly issued her own, much less civil, adios.

The shrill jangle of the telephone jolted Dee back to the present.

"Hello?" Even to herself she sounded faint.

"Dee, honey? Is that you? Are you all right?" Felicia's concerned voice filled Dee's ear.

Dee cleared her throat and tried again. "Yeah. I'm okay."

Felicia's disbelief flooded the phone line. "You are most decidedly not okay. And what are you doing home in the middle of the day?"

"It's a long story."

"Is it those police detectives? What have they been doing to you? I have half a mind to go down to their captain and give them a royal going over. I can't believe how they hassle innocent, law-abiding people when there are criminals, really dangerous criminals, out there wandering the streets free and easy, never having to worry…"

Dee cut in. "No, it's not the police. It's morose thoughts."

"Morose? That's not the Dee I know." Felicia paused. "Well now, girlfriend, I have just the cure for them blues. You asked me for a haircut last week and I was just calling to arrange one. Since you're free, why don't you come on by my place now and I'll trim you all up while you explain just how you came by this leisure time?"

"It's not a pretty story."

Felicia laughed. "I'd only be surprised if it were."

Chapter 10

"Girlfriend, you are jumpier than a bullfrog at a python convention. You can't tell me that this is all bad thoughts. Whatever is going on with you?"

Dee paused her fidgeting long enough to allow Felicia to safely continue cutting her hair. She leaned back into the old dentist chair which Felicia had installed in one corner of her huge kitchen for use with her private clients. The lattice windows on two walls of the room gave Felicia the natural light she needed while offering her patrons a view of her water garden.

Dee shifted her hips while trying to hold her head still. "I've just been running circles in my head over who would want Sheila dead. Her ex-husband is quite a hothead, so why would he wait seven years to get his revenge? Is Rachel really a lover being two-timed? Seems a pretty weak excuse to do someone in. Did Curtis find out about Sheila and Rachel and get his male ego damaged? Seems like a lame reason for bashing her head in. I need a nice, solid, believable motive like money, revenge or at least fame."

Felicia paused in mid snip. "That could be it."

"What could?"

"The station's undergoing a shift in philosophy. You know, no more all bad. Emphasize the good." She placed her fists on her slim hips. "It's like the bloodhound and the hare."

"I'll bite. Which hare is that?"

"The old bloodhound is guarding the garden. He knows a

hare's been chomping on the carrots, so he's sniffing and sniffing after the hare, but the hare's already in his burrow. By the time the bloodhound finds the hole, that hare's back in the garden having a picnic on the lettuce."

"And the network is...?"

"The bloodhound of course. The public's the hare. The station's always sniffing after what the public wants so they can change the format and appeal to the widest audience. By the time they find out what the newest trend is..."

"The hare's gone on to a new trend."

"Exactly." Felicia poised her scissors again.

"What I don't know is how a woman born and raised in San Pedro, California, comes up with all these country analogies."

"Heritage, girlfriend. If you grew up with grandparents from South Carolina and parents from Georgia, you'd quote country wisdom, too."

Dee paused in thought as Felicia resumed the trim. "So you think the change in format caused Sheila's death?"

"I'm not sure how, but it's a shakeup that might effect a lot of jobs." Snip. "I don't think it has to do with her being gay. She came out three years ago." Snip.

"Everyone knows?"

"All the network brass. You know those good old boys were none too pleased, but her numbers were too high to cut her."

Dee glanced over to the mirror perched on the kitchen counter. She focused on her reflection and her quickly shortening hair. "Speaking of cutting, are we aiming for a gender-bending look here?"

Felicia tilted her head. She met Dee's look in the mirror and grinned. "You'd probably look real cute with shaved sides, but I guess that's out, huh?"

"'Fraid so. If I ever get to return to teaching, that kind of look may cause a stir. And I know my principal is not as open-minded as the network execs."

Felicia nodded and combed through the now very short

curly brown hair once more checking for long wisps. As she snipped an errant strand she said, "I can't believe any of these people around here would kill Sheila, not even for her job. Of course, I don't know them as well as she did. It's too bad we can't read her book."

"I forgot about her book. She never mentioned it to me. When did she start talking about it?"

Felicia considered for a moment. "I guess it was right after she moved to the five o'clock news. She said something about more free time now and how she'd had this thought running through her head for awhile."

"Wait a minute. Who knew about this book?" Dee's tone was sharp as she straightened in her chair.

"Why, everyone seems to have. I mean, honey, Sheila was many things, but modest was not one of them. Since she mentioned it to me while she was getting her hair styled at the station, I'm guessing she wasn't too particular about who overheard her."

"Did she say what was going to be in it?"

"Not exactly. But she hinted about how lots of people would be surprised." Felicia's dark eyes grew wide. "Are you thinking someone…?"

"I think it's entirely possible that someone didn't want her to write that book. I wonder what secrets she was going to let out. Do you have any clues?"

"Well, now, she did say that she wanted to include all the people in her life, famous or not. She said she wanted people to know her real life, not just the glitz."

Dee paled. "Oh my God. Do you think I'm in it?"

"Why? Worried you maiden aunt in Barcelona might faint?"

"I think the authorities might consider it an additional motive, don't you? Which might explain why they've been picking on me."

Felicia dropped her arms and stared at Dee. "Lordy. I didn't think of that."

"Maybe I'll be lucky and there's something truly terrible about someone else in it." Dee got out of the leather chair and bent over, vigorously brushing her hands through her now two-inch long hair. Curly wisps of brown flew over the surrounding floor.

Felicia plopped into the recently vacated seat. "What if the police don't have it? What if the killer does?"

Dee looked upside down at her friend. She straightened her back one vertebra at a time. "Pierce mentioned that Sheila's apartment was trashed and her computer was destroyed. What if Sheila was murdered to get that manuscript?" She lapsed into thought. "Wouldn't the murderer be shocked if there just happened to be another copy around?"

"You aren't thinking…"

"Why not? I'm certainly not getting anywhere except closer to a jail cell by playing the sleuth. Maybe going on the offensive might be the way to stir things up."

"Stir things up, girl? Stir things up? We are talking about a killer—someone who bashes people over the head—someone who ends a life—someone who—"

"Now hold on. We're not exactly talking Jeffrey Dalmer here. Maybe this was a spur of the moment thing. Maybe the person's really sorry."

"Oh, yeah. So sorry he's going to just throw up his hands and confess because he didn't happen to get every single copy of what Sheila wrote? Are you nuts?"

Dee crossed her arms. "Tully would do it."

"Girl, we already know Tully's nuts. It's your sanity I'm questioning."

"Are you going to help or not?"

"Not. I don't want to attend another funeral anytime soon. Especially yours."

Dee placed both hands on the arms of the chair and swiveled it so Felicia was facing her. A look from green eyes bore into dark ones. "They are going to arrest me. I have no alibi.

They have an eyewitness who swears I was there that night. My fingerprints are all over the condo. The police don't believe we had a friendly break-up. And they sure as hell won't believe that I wouldn't care if my name were plastered all over a best seller as a lesbian. I will be damned if I go quietly into that good night, as it were. So," she said, leaning closer, "will you help me or not?"

Felicia stared straight ahead, silent. Several moments passed before she sighed and pulled herself out of the chair. Looking down into Dee's face, she shook her head. "Jenny's at work, so she can't help. We'd better go call Tully."

"How about billboards?" Much to Felicia's dismay, Tully's reception of Dee's plan was enthusiastic, if not practical. "Too obvious?"

"A touch." Dee flopped back on Felicia's couch and propped her white, unblemished tennis shoes on the coffee table. "I had something a bit more subtle in mind."

Felicia paced the width of her living room. She stopped her strides long enough to shake her head at Dee. "Girlfriend, you need a keeper. In fact, you both need keepers." She turned to face Tully. "When Dee told me about this lame-brained scheme, I thought we should at least know where to find her body. Now I have the both of you to worry about."

"Aw shucks, Felicia. Too bad you didn't realize our latent insanity before you became friends with us." Tully winked at Dee. "All right, my pragmatic partner, we tell the world about this manuscript. Who has it? Where? How did she get it? Has she read it? Let's get our stories, if you'll pardon the expression, straight."

The three friends decided to release just the notion that Dee had a copy which she had partially read. Vagueness seemed the best approach. "After all," Dee concluded, "if Sheila had given me a copy, I probably wouldn't even have mentioned it to you guys."

Felicia rolled her eyes. "Honey child, you would have been

on the phone two minutes later reading chapter one out loud."

Dee blushed. "Yeah, well, everyone doesn't have to know that."

"So, I'll spread it around the community," Tully said, "While Felicia tells the world of television, and you tell our friends." She breathed deeply. "Then we all sit around until the old horse manure strikes the air conditioning unit."

"Maybe nothing will happen." Dee sounded depressed.

"With your luck lately, I wouldn't count on it."

Chapter 11

"I need to consult with you on a professional basis." Dee attempted to make her voice sound calm and rational.

Evie paused before replying. "I'm glad you've decided to seek help, but I wouldn't be the right person for the job. I could give you a referral if you'd like."

"No, wait!" Dee realized she was sending Evie the wrong message. Throughout their year together, Evie had urged Dee to try psychotherapy. Dee's obstinate refusals finally silenced Evie, but Dee now understood that rather than ending the subject, it had just sent the topic underground. "I want to talk with you. It's about your impressions—your professional impressions—of some of the people in Sheila's life. I need a handle on this. I don't know where else to turn."

"You just want my opinions about these people?"

"Yeah." Dee nodded her head at the receiver. "I need help with motives and reactions and possible abnormal signs."

"I am not a criminologist."

"Some of those kids you deal with border on the criminal." Dee hastened onward, before Evie could begin an ardent defense of the maladjusted juveniles who populated her social skills group. "I think you're a great judge of character and you seem to understand how people tick. That's all I want. Your insight."

Negotiations ended with an agreement to meet for an early dinner (not, under any circumstances, to be misconstrued as a date) with Dee paying, since this was a consultation. Dee hung up the phone exhausted, but more pleased than a paid parlance might warrant.

Throwing her arms above her head and stretching past her five feet four inches, Dee felt her shoulders pop as some of the tension of the past week ebbed. Laundry, dusting, vacuuming, and gardening vied for her attention. Instead she decided on a walk. Lake Hollywood reservoir was a favorite loop. She figured a Friday morning might be the perfect time for a solitary stroll.

Dee turned off Wonder View Drive and curbed the wheels of her Hyundai on the steep incline of Lake Hollywood Drive which led to the north gate of the three and one half mile walking path. Technically, the street and cement path around the reservoir weren't just for walking. Joggers and people on bicycles, skates, and skateboards frequented the trail as well. But Dee loved to stroll beside the pine and eucalyptus trees which ringed part of the fenced off reservoir. The birds, trees, wildflowers, and ever-changing colors of the lake made the setting too peaceful to hurry past.

Dee set a twenty-minute-mile pace and strode up the side street leading to the fenced-in path. She pumped her bent arms to increase the workout to her heart. The warmth of the sun on her shoulders and the steady beat of her feet freed her mind to wander.

She debated the wisdom of her decision to announce her supposed ownership of the manuscript. She wondered about Tully's progress with Gina Quinn. Flights of fantasy filled her head about the night's meeting with Evie. Then Dee's thoughts darkened as the parade of murder suspects marched through her mind.

Which was when she ran into Lurch.

At first she dismissed her identification of Steve Montgomery. Too much brooding and not enough food. But the more she gained on the tall, lanky fellow, the more convinced she was that it was Sheila's ex-husband.

Minus a plan of attack, she called out, "Hi!"

The man looked neither right nor left. He wasn't out for a power walk, but his stroll was fast enough to make Dee breathe hard in her efforts to reach him.

She pulled alongside him and discovered the reason for his unresponsiveness. A Walkman and earphones. Undaunted, she waved her hand and repeated her greeting, only louder.

Steve Montgomery smiled. Dee was amazed by what a change that smile made in him. It had charm and warmth and intimacy all wrapped into white teeth and crinkling eyes. She found herself drawn into the depths of his gray eyes, eyes that had seemed cold and void at the Shelbourne's home now held a welcoming twinkle.

It took a moment for Dee to register that he had spoken and was now looking at her, waiting for a response. She blushed. "Sorry. I didn't catch what you said."

He laughed. "I'm used to students dozing off, but only after I've lectured for half an hour."

"You're a teacher."

He nodded, sliding the headband down around his neck. "A professor actually. At San Diego State. I'm Steve Montgomery." He stuck out his hand.

"Dee DelValle," Dee said as she met his grasp. "What's a San Diego professor doing wandering Lake Hollywood?"

Steve grinned. "I'm on sabbatical this semester. I've rented a condo in North Hollywood and a neighbor recommended this place for my walks."

"Smart neighbor. What's your field?"

"Biology. Physiology and anatomy are my main interests, but I pinch hit in other areas as well."

"I'm a teacher, too. My target audience is a little younger than yours, but I bet there aren't a lot of other differences."

The two had started walking along the stony trail, stepping aside when three bicyclists raced by. As they walked under the hillside of the famed Hollywood sign, they exchanged professional horror stories.

Dee and Steve passed the east gate and started across the dam. Midway, they paused at the monument erected by the City of Los Angeles Department of Public Works to commemorate the construction of the Hollywood Reservoir in December of 1924. Dee was quite familiar with the bronze plaque since her ancestor, Reginald DelValle, was one of the Commissioners listed on it.

Dee and Steve leaned against the handrails of the dam and squirted water down their throats from their sports bottles. Dee tried to bring the subject around to Sheila.

"I remember seeing you at Sheila Shelbourne's funeral."

Steve's eyes clouded over and he turned to look out over the lake. "So that's where I've seen you before." His voice flattened.

"I didn't mean to upset you."

Steve shook his head. "You didn't. I guess I'm still amazed to think of Sheila as being dead. She was so very alive." He turned to face Dee again. "But I guess you know that."

"Yes." Dee decided a minimal answer would serve her better than any detailed recitation. "Did you start your sabbatical?"

"No. I've been up here a few months now. I'm doing some research at USC and UCLA using their hospitals and medical libraries. I'm doing a study of recent experiments regarding the treatment of macular degeneration."

While Steve launched into a rather detailed account of retinas and wet and dry forms of the disease, Dee split her brain between showing the proper amount of attention to his dissertation and trying to come up with a scheme for getting more information about Sheila.

"So," Dee interjected while Steve paused for water, "did you get time to visit with Sheila before...well, before..."

"Before she was killed?" Steve shook his head. "No. We weren't on visiting terms."

"Oh?"

Steve shrugged. "Sheila and I were married. And we got

divorced. It wasn't nasty, but it wasn't friendly either."

"Yet you were at her funeral."

Steve shrugged again. "I've kept in touch with her folks. They're good people, no matter what Sheila says."

They started down the last leg of the Lake Hollywood trail. With time short, Dee decided to probe. "I can't imagine staying in touch with my ex-in-laws. Didn't that create some tension between Sheila and her parents?"

Steve shook his head. "Sheila wasn't that close to her parents. She and her father had never gotten along and she blamed her mom for taking Henry's side."

"So you three shared an anger towards Sheila."

Dee's comment stopped Steve's steps. His gray eyes became as cool as the dark waters of the lake. "What do you mean by that?"

"Just that they must have been hurt by Sheila's rejection of them and you must have been angry about how things turned out between the two of you, with her leaving you and everything."

"What makes you think Sheila left me?" The gray eyes were now ice.

Dee looked about. No joggers approached. No children on bicycles rode laughing by. The other fitness seekers had disappeared just when she wanted them most. She started walking in the hopes Steve Montgomery would automatically follow. "Oh, I guess it was just one of those rumors I heard flying by." He rejoined her and she increased her pace.

Steve grunted, as if satisfied. "Rumors. There certainly were a lot of them around Sheila."

"I know they bothered Sheila," Dee agreed, knowing no such thing. "I bet that's why she decided to write her book."

"Book? What book?" Steve sounded puzzled.

"Didn't you know? Sheila was writing her autobiography."

An inscrutable looked passed over Steve's face and he did not respond. Dee puzzled without success over his sudden withdrawal as they headed down the last stretch of the reserve's jogging path.

They reached Weidlake Gate, the exit of the loop, without further discussion. When Dee saw people and cars and the relative safety of civilization, she decided to push the issue. "I've read part of Sheila's manuscript. She wrote well."

"You've actually seen this book?"

"She gave me a copy. I haven't had time to read it all yet, but I plan to get to it soon."

Steve stared off into the distance then wiped his forehead with a shirtsleeve. "I'm sure her parents would be interested to have that."

"That's a great idea. Maybe I'll send it to them after I finish."

They stretched their bodies in silence. Dee put out her legs one at a time against the cement blocks that held the gate poles guarding the lake's pathway. She rotated her ankles. She waited for Steve to make the next move.

When she looked over at him, he smiled, the warmth once again radiating from his eyes. "It was nice having company on the walk. How about getting a cool drink somewhere? Maybe you can tell me about other places to hike around here."

"Thanks, but I have to get back. I've got an appointment in a little bit and I've got to clean up first."

"Oh." His voice held disappointment then his face lightened. "Maybe we could get together another time? Why don't you give me your phone number and I'll give you a call?"

"That wouldn't be a good idea. I'm involved with someone."

"He's a lucky guy."

Dee decided to let that one pass. She stopped at her car and turned to Steve. "Thanks for the company."

"My pleasure. Do you live around here? Maybe we'll run into each other sometime."

"I live in Burbank, so I'm not too far away. Maybe we'll meet here again sometime."

Relationships Can Be Murder

Dee glanced into her rear view mirror as she drove away. Steve Montgomery stood, staring after her. Somehow, she didn't think it was her feminine allure that drew his fervent interest.

Chapter 12

Casa Carina in Silverlake was one of the original gay-friendly establishments of that community. The structure had been the owner's house, which he remodeled into a restaurant. When the restaurant had opened, thirty years before, the bathroom's pedestal sink was left in the center of what was now the dining room, its bowl filled with dirt and planted with flowers. The sink was long gone, but the original floor plan was still discernible.

Dee parked her own car, five-thirty being much too early for the valet service. She was pleased to note Evie's silver sports car two spots over from hers. It was easy to spot since there were only five other cars in the whole lot.

Dee climbed the stairs of what used to be the back porch and entered the dining room. She stopped when she saw Evie. Someone entered behind Dee causing a sudden breeze to flow from the open windows by Evie's table out the restaurant's open door. Dee felt herself blown backwards eleven months in time.

They had had their first date at Casa Carina, and Evie, with her black, shiny hair and serious eyes had waited for Dee at that same table. The butterflies then were due to the excitement of fulfilling a fantasy which had consumed Dee for three long months.

Last year, Dee had the challenge of Robert Kilmer in class. Robert had the IQ of any three of her other students combined and the social graces of an elephant at high tea. Her struggles to help him win friends and influence enemies only netted him the label of teacher's pet.

His parents, Mr. and Mrs. Kilmer, were equally frustrated, or perhaps even more. After all, they had had ten years with the boy. When Dee suggested counseling, they had agreed with enthusiasm.

Through friends and the lesbian network of therapists which functioned well in L.A., Dee heard about Evelyn Taylor, an MSW, who specialized in the development of adolescent social skills.

One requirement Evie had for working with Robert was that his teacher be part of the program. Dee was none too thrilled with this prerequisite but yielded to the pressure from the Kilmers and from Robert's continued maladjustment at school.

Evie's voice during the first telephone conference piqued Dee's interest. Their first meeting grabbed the attention of the rest of her body.

Throughout this face-to-face consultation, Evie discussed possible intervention techniques for use with Robert. Meanwhile, Dee kept trying to figure out how to ask Evie out.

Dee's eventual overtures were met with a firm rejection.

"I am involved in this case as a professional." Evie had informed Dee. "As are you. Robert is our only reason for contact as long as he remains in your class."

Dee took that to mean there would be hope once school was over. She bided her time until June. Robert left her class with excellent grades and one developing friendship. Dee then called Evie to ask her out to dinner. To Dee's relief, Evie had accepted.

First dates were not Dee's favorite. She had endured four in the preceding six months. Joanne had given an endless recitation of her ex-lovers' faults. Trudy had offered a list of her own failings. Deanna had analyzed why both she and Dee were still single at their advanced ages. And Carmen had so poked and prodded that Dee felt she would be asked to open wide while

Carmen counted the fillings in her teeth. There had been no encores with any of those women.

At Dee and Evie's first date, the evening had progressed in a different manner. Evie hadn't volunteered her history of involvements, made no disclaimers, offered no psychological insights. Instead she had laughed at Dee's stories of students' antics and shared a few moments of therapy humor (client anonymous) of her own. They discussed travel and books and movies and coming-out stories. They had left that night with a warm hug at their cars and a date for the next week.

The slam of the restaurant's door yanked Dee to the present. Evie's looked over to where Dee was rooted. No welcoming smile lit Evie's face. Dee's fantasies fled as reality crept in.

"Hey." Dee's voice sounded feeble, even to herself. "Thanks for agreeing to meet me."

"After all you've been through it's the least I can do."

As she slid into the vinyl seat, Dee mulled over the comment, trying to find deeper meanings. She failed. "Are you here because you're sorry for me or here because you still care, at least a little?"

Evie's eyes grew until they mimicked the shape of her glasses' round lens. Before she could respond, a rather rotund waitress sauntered by to take their drink and dinner orders.

Libations accounted for, the two women faced each other over the vast emotional expanse of the last few months.

Evie crossed her arms on the table and leaned forward. "I don't know whether to be impressed or appalled by your question."

"Do I get a vote?"

The dead silence that greeted her gave Dee the feeling that Evie wasn't quite ready for her humor.

"In answer to your first question, I came because you asked for my professional help. Since I do know some of the people involved and I also deal with some clients who are, perhaps minorly, antisocial personalities, I felt I might be able to lend a hand. As a therapist. As a humane individual. Not as a lover."

"Oh." Dee felt her chest constrict. Daunted, she nevertheless decided to salvage what she could of their meeting. She drummed the table with both hands. "OK, now that the ground rules are set, let me tell you what I know."

Over Margaritas, Dee filled Evie in on her activities of the last week. Evie chewed on the edge of a tortilla chip as her eyes lost focus and she slumped back in the booth. Dee recognized Evie's thinking mode and kept silent.

Just as Dee licked the last spot of salt off the rim of her glass, Evie's focus returned to the room. "A couple of thoughts. First of all, what about the father?"

"Sheila's dad? What do you mean, what about him?"

"Why did her ex-husband say Sheila and her father didn't get along? In fact, it must have exceeded not getting along since Sheila not only distanced herself from her father, but was also angry with her mother for not defending her."

"I don't think Steve said Sheila's mother didn't defend her. I think it was more like sides of an argument."

Evie slid her glasses partway down her nose and stared at Dee. "One doesn't stop speaking to one's primary care givers over a simple argument." She pushed her glasses back up with her index finger. "Sounds like abuse to me."

"Abuse? Like in sexual molestation?"

Evie nodded. "It could be sexual, but it just as well may be physical or emotional abuse. That would shed some light on her drive for perfection. Sexual abuse would explain her promiscuity and her inability to form monogamous relationships."

"Lots of people have trouble with that who haven't been the least bit abused."

Evie raised her eyebrows. "At least you're not trying to use that particular excuse."

The rotund waitress interrupted what would have been a scathing response by Dee, once Dee had thought of one. The steaming plate of Arroz con Pollo distracted her. She heaped on extra salsa and hot sauce. The pleasant fire in her mouth made the temptation of fiery speech dissipate. She decided to take the high road.

"Isn't it a pretty big leap to say she was abused just from that one comment of her ex?"

Evie, her mouth filled with Chile Relleno, shook her head. She swallowed. "It's not the comment. It's the pattern. As for what type of abuse it was, I can't make a guess without other information."

"Like what?"

"Like what Sheila was like in bed, how she made love and what she would and would not do."

Dee choked on her chicken. "We are not going there."

"I understand. I was just making the point that there are patterns of behavior for women who have been sexually abused and so I cannot form an hypothesis just from what you've told me."

"OK," Dee said, "you think there was abuse of one form or another." She held up one hand before Evie's protest could leave her lips. "You think there possibly was incest or emotional abuse." She chewed a piece of chicken and added more hot sauce to her dish before continuing. "That would make Sheila's book a threat to Mr. Shelbourne. But would the impending exposure be enough of a motive for a person like him to kill his own daughter?"

"That may be an avenue of investigation for you. Has he a police record? Does he have any history of violence, domestic or otherwise? It sounds as if Tully might have the police connection to get that checked out."

"I'm not sure how much of that connection is wishful thinking on her part."

"Tully is being wishful about someone else?" Evie sounded amused. "My, how some things change."

Dee grinned. "It is kind of nice seeing the shoe on the other foot for a change." She finished the last drop of her Margarita and then asked, "What was the other thing you thought of?"

"Never underestimate the emasculating power of a lesbian relationship."

Dee tilted her head. "You think there may be a wounded male ego involved?"

"Maybe more than one. And when a male has been symbolically castrated, all hell can break loose."

Chapter 13

"Rachel doesn't do drugs, but she seems to be a social drinker." The next day Felicia faced Dee and Tully over Dee's glass and oak coffee table. Tully had a list in front of her and they were running down the names of Channel 8 personnel looking for weaknesses. "And Curtis doesn't drink. At least not much."

"Really?" Dee sounded skeptical. "He was pretty blotto at Sheila's wake. In fact, I'd say he was three out of four sheets to the wind."

Felicia raised her eyebrows. "I've never seen him have more than one glass of wine. Maybe he hates funerals as much as I do."

"True. I was tempted to down a few myself that day." Dee leaned forward. "But what did he have to be so upset about? He should have been happy. He and Sheila obviously didn't get along."

Felicia grunted. "It was beyond not getting along. One time Curtis cut Sheila's spot by thirty seconds to cover a slow speed chase on the Ventura freeway. During the commercial break, Sheila managed to call Curtis a sleazy idiot and impugned his parentage without once using a curse word."

"That must have caused his undies to bunch. How did he deal with that? Wasn't he her boss?"

"Only in some ways. Directors lay out story order, camera angles, and other technical logistics like when to break away for on-the-spot coverage. He also has a say in certain matters like allocation of time to reports and who gets assigned to various investigations. But the anchors are pretty much invincible to anyone except the network brass. Those are the ones who hire and fire."

Tully said, "Maybe Sheila had something on him. Maybe she was blackmailing him and he killed her."

Dee considered that as she reached for a carrot stick.

The women had all contributed snacks to share since Tully had declared that brainstorming burned up calories at an accelerated rate. Dee's first choice would have been Felicia's homemade chocolate chip cookies, but her scale that morning had been unkind. She struggled to pull her thoughts away from the beckoning sugar.

"Maybe. But they have worked together for some time now. If she were blackmailing him, why would he choose to kill her now?" Dee crunched her carrot.

"Maybe the blackmailing just started." Felicia shared none of Dee's food phobias. She slipped one of the chocolate chip cookies into her mouth.

Tully put her boots on the oak rim of the coffee table and leaned back into the cushions. "That's a whole lot of maybes and not a lot of for sures."

Dee started to run her fingers through her hair then stopped when she realized the lack of length gave her nothing to grab. Frustrated, she marched over to the refrigerator and dragged out the sun tea jar to replenish her drink. "All we really know for sure is that Sheila was murdered for a reason."

"No, good buddy." Tully thumped a boot on the floor. "The only thing we know for sure is the police are still after your cute little rear. The rest is an educated guess."

Dee set her glass on the tile counter top with a bare click. "All right, physical evidence: none. First hand knowledge: limited. Suppositions: unbounded. And no overt reaction from anyone about the book."

Tully shook her head. "Most people seemed only mildly interested. A couple said they had heard something about Sheila writing a book, but they weren't women who had been involved with her."

Felicia concurred. "No one at the studio fainted dead away or clutched her hand to her throat at the thought. But then lots of people knew she was at least talking about writing one. You know she wasn't shy about self-promotion."

Felicia stopped pacing and snapped her fingers. "Maybe we need to make a time line. You know, trace everyone's whereabouts and alibis and what all. We're not getting anywhere on motive, so why not look at means?"

Agreeing that anything was better than flogging the current dead horse, Dee marched into her office. She brought out a flip chart and wrote the information on the board as Tully read from her note pad. The teacher in Dee emerged as she listed collaborated evidence in red, single witness testimony in blue, hearsay and rumor in green, and her own information in black.

"Are we leaving anything out?" Dee stepped back to study the colorful chart.

"Didn't I tell you?" Felicia pointed to Steve Montgomery's name on the board. "He was at the station that Friday."

Tully sighed. "No, little lady, you happened to leave that out of your report. Why in blazes didn't you tell us this before?"

Felicia's hands flew into the air. "First of all, I didn't know who he was when he showed up at the station. Secondly, I was never introduced to him at Sheila's wake. Third, it wasn't until today that I got that the guy you keep calling Lurch and Sheila's ex were one and the same. And it wasn't until just now that I remembered where I had seen Lurch before."

Dee intervened. "Will you two get a grip? Felicia, I don't care where or when you made the connection, I want to know why this guy, who supposedly hadn't seen Sheila since the divorce, was at the studio."

"He was asking about Sheila, where she was and all. But all

anyone knew was that she had taken the day off for personal reasons," Felicia said, sliding into a wicker chair. "Which is another strange thing."

"What do you mean?" Dee was filling in Steve's visit on the chart.

"Anchors never take time off. Not unless they're on special assignment. They don't want to risk the fill-in doing a better job."

"Insecure bunch." Tully shook her head. "But if Sheila wasn't there that day, how did Lurch get on the set? And did he ever find out where Sheila was?"

Felicia shrugged. "Guess the only way we'll ever know that is if we lie down with the dogs, so to speak."

Dee groaned. "I don't even want to guess at a translation for that one."

Felicia crossed her legs. "You know the old saying. If you lie down with dogs, you'll get up with fleas."

"Am I to take that to mean you want one of us to spend time with Mr. Montgomery and in close enough proximity to catch his diseases?" Dee sniffed. "Count me out. I vote for Tully."

"Now, good buddy, I know you've got no history with men, but I don't think Felicia was suggesting sexual relations. Lunch would probably do."

"Why me?" Dee threw the pen on the easel's chalk tray. "If Kinsey Millhone had me for a partner, her series would have ended with A."

Tully's drawl took on a soft tone. "I know you're not really keen on this, Dee, but you're the only one he knows. He'd probably think it's a little strange if Felicia, Jenny, or I called him up and asked to see him."

Dee chewed her lower lip. She considered the options. Life in prison verses lunch with Lurch. Even that comparison didn't make the prospect more appealing.

"All right. If you two figure a way for me to contact him that doesn't make me sound hot for his hairy body, I'll do it." She picked up the pen. "But let's finish with what we already know. What time was he poking around the set?"

Felicia thought. "I'd say around three o'clock. We were gearing up for the four o'clock show and Fernando, the assistant director, was frantic. Sheila was off, he couldn't find Curtis, and he was afraid he'd end up being in charge of the show. Into the chaos walks this huge guy with a suit and a fedora, looking cool and gorgeous. Half the women on the floor stopped to drool."

"Lurch? Gorgeous?" Tully snorted.

"He wasn't looking his best at the funeral." Dee shrugged. "He really is good looking—for a man."

Tully raised one eyebrow, but did not reply.

Dee wrote on the chart using black since she figured Felicia's direct evidence was as good as her own. She studied the chart again for holes.

"So now we know Steve was in the area and had enough time to make it over to Sheila's condo to kill her. But we don't know about Sheila's dad."

Tully jumped in. "We also don't know about Curtis Lee. Didn't you just say the A.D. couldn't find Curtis before the four o'clock show?"

"I know he was looking for Curtis when Stunning Steve walked in, but I don't know if he found him later." Felicia swiped a piece of paper from Tully's notebook and started writing. "I'll check on that and I'll also find out if anyone told Steve where to find Sheila." She grinned. "The old bloodhound is on the trail."

"OK, then I'll see what I can find out about the history of one Mr. Henry Shelbourne. If he's violent, somebody will know. Even in an upscale neighborhood like the Palisades there's got to be at least one nosy neighbor. Maybe they'll even know where he was that Friday. And let me take the chart with me, I'll put it on my computer and make copies for all of us." Tully inscribed her assignment and nodded. She stood and reached for Felicia's hand. "Come on compadre. We've got work to do."

Dee handed Tully the chart and followed them out to their

cars. Felicia hopped in her car and drove away with a wave. Tully then walked over to a green coupe, unlocked the door, and tossed in the color-coded chart.

Dee stopped and stared at the car. Blood rose in her cheeks. "Tully," she asked, her voice tight, "where's your Jeep?"

"In the shop. Jenny let me borrow hers for today."

"I thought Jenny's Honda was blue."

Tully paused as she regarded the car and then looked at Dee. Her smile seemed forced. "She just bought this one a few days ago."

Dee stared after Tully as she drove away in Jenny's new dark green Honda. With a gay pride license plate holder on the back.

Chapter 14

"You don't look surprised to see me," Dee commented as Jenny led the way into her living room that evening. Dee loved Jenny's house. It was a Greene and Greene California bungalow which Jenny had restored to its original 1920s grandeur. The wooden floors gleamed with polish and the exposed oak beams of the ceiling were dark with oil. In contrast to the house, all the furnishings were light and contemporary. Dee could never imagine having Jenny's brilliance in allowing the two decades to serve as a perfect complement to each other.

Jenny slid her tall, broad body elegantly into one of the two modern Swedish chairs that flanked a small stone fireplace. "Tully called me at work and told me you'd probably be showing up soon."

"She warned you."

"She warned me. You might even say she strongly suggested I not be around when you got here."

"You obviously didn't take her advice. Why?"

Jenny shrugged her broad shoulders and crossed one ankle over the other. "I'm not about to leave town to avoid you. Plus there are some things you have the right to know."

"So you were at Sheila's condo that night. And Tully knew." Dee felt an equal mix of anger and sorrow.

Jenny shook her head. "Tully didn't know. Not then. She did not find out until today when you made such a point of my car. Don't blame Tully; I strained her loyalties. She just did what she could."

Dee struggled with her emotions. Jenny was her friend, and Tully was her best friend. Knowing they had such a trust between them of which she knew nothing filled Dee with envy and hurt. But would Tully really lie to protect a murderer? And could Jenny really commit such a crime?

Jenny shared Dee's silence, but her angular face reflected no hint of what she might be thinking.

Dee's anger burst through. "Why the hell didn't you tell me?"

Jenny shrugged again. "Since I saw your car that day, I figured you had spotted mine. But then you never brought it up."

Dee felt more confused than ever. If Jenny had spotted her car, then that meant Jenny had arrived after Dee, while Sheila had still been alive. Did Jenny see the killer?"Did you see me leave Sheila's condo?"

Jenny shook her head. "No. I spotted your car when I drove up. I parked a little in front of you and tried to figure out what to do. Quite frankly, I didn't relish the thought of confronting Sheila with you there. Since I didn't know if you were there for the moment or for the night, I took a walk to calm down. When I got back, your car was gone."

"So you assumed the coast was clear."

Jenny nodded.

Dee stared at her friend then switched her gaze to the empty fireplace. Despite the warm weather, she wished for a fire to burn away her doubts and add some normalcy to this conversation. But no flames soothed her or brightened her dark thoughts. Still not looking at Jenny she asked, "You went up to see her?"

A bare nod was the only response.

"Did anyone come out of the condo building before you went in?"

Jenny did not seem fazed by Dee's lack of eye contact. "I did not notice anyone."

"How about when you entered the hall?"

Again a negative.

"Were there any sounds from her condo when you got there?"

"Nothing."

Dee swung her eyes back to meet Jenny's. Jenny's blue eyes, fringed with mascara, stared back without blinking. As much as Dee liked her friend, she still had to ask. "Did you kill Sheila?"

Jenny ran her large right hand up and down her left arm as if smoothing away a chill. "No. She was dead when I got there." Holding up a manicured finger she stopped Dee's comment before it could leave her mouth. "I know it sounds like a B movie, but my timing was so incredibly bad that night. Too late to save her, too late to see the murderer, too late to do anything except incriminate myself."

"How do you know she was dead? Did you see her?"

"When I got to her door, it was open, but the room was dark." Jenny's eyes closed as she continued her recital. "I reached over to turn on the lamp. It wasn't there. I thought maybe I hadn't reached far enough, or she had redecorated, or whatever, but when I walked forward, I stubbed my toe on something. I moved it out of the way and found the lamp—her beautiful Tiffany lamp—on its side on the floor. I set it upright and turned on the light."

"I couldn't believe the place! Books all over the floor, tables overturned, her gorgeous brass bookshelf on the ground. And that's when I saw Sheila." Jenny grew still and pale. "One look and I knew." She shook her head.

Dee tried to capture Jenny's look, but Jenny was hunched over, staring at her clasped hands. Wavering between belief and disbelief, Dee sat in silence. It all seemed so unlikely. As far as Dee knew, Jenny never associated with Sheila. She shouldn't have even known where Sheila lived, let alone have shown up there to talk to her on a Friday night. "I don't get it. Why were you there? How did you know Sheila?"

Jenny smiled, but it was a smile that held no pleasure. "How did I know Sheila? In much the same way you did, I'd guess."

Dee's jaw bounced on her kneecaps. "You? You and Sheila? The two of you had an affair? But you're known for being, you know…And Sheila was so…"

"So I was the chaste-nun type while she was the party girl."

Dee blushed and stammered a bit. "Well, something like that."

Jenny seemed unperturbed by her reputation. "Maybe that's what intrigued Sheila. And she was definitely intrigued. She kept after me for three months. Invitations, compliments, flowers." Jenny's gaze drifted to the beamed ceiling. "I'm still not sure why I gave in to her. But it ended almost as soon as it started. I guess when the immovable object jumps, the irresistible force loses interest."

"When did all this happen?"

"About a year ago."

"A year ago? Then why all of a sudden did you go to Sheila's Friday?" Dee frowned. "Unless the two of you were picking up where you left off?"

"God, no." Jenny's emphasis left no doubt in Dee's mind. It echoed her own sentiments too closely. "No, I went because Sheila called me to tell me about her upcoming book."

"Her book?" Dee's momentary delight in having got something right faded as she realized that this motive was not one she had linked to Jenny. "Why did you want to see her about her book?"

"I wanted to talk her out of including me."

"How did you know you'd be in it? And why do you care?"

Jenny shifted on the cushion then started to stand. "Maybe Tully was right. This wasn't a good idea after all." She straightened herself and looked down at Dee who was still entrenched in the other chair. "Look, I told you that you were right. I was at Sheila's place that night. And I've told you why. And I'm also telling you again, I didn't kill her."

"OK," Dee said, still seated. "I won't push. But don't you think the police will want more? They're going to find the same trail we did."

"They'll get the same answers."

Dee stood and faced Jenny. She searched the smooth cheeks, cleft chin, and thickly-lashed, round eyes for the person she thought she knew. "We've been friends for over three years. You even tried to warn me off when I started to get involved with Sheila. Why can't we work together on this?"

"I have been working with you."

"The hell you have. You've been lying to me and misleading me."

"When? What did I ever say that was a lie?"

Dee floundered. "Well, it was a sin of omission then."

"I don't know I'd say it was a sin. But you've got to know that I would never withhold anything that could help you prove your innocence. Nor would I tell the police anything that would strengthen their case."

On her way home, Dee began to wonder if that was a promise, or a threat.

Chapter 15

Dee jogged through the cool Sunday morning air. The regularity of her feet hitting the sidewalk of the tree-shaded block of Clark Street always allowed her mind to wander. Today her thoughts dwelt in a frightening land: a land where Tully and Jenny kept secrets from her; a land where Sheila Shelbourne knew something about Jenny that Dee didn't; a land where her best friends and lovers were people she really didn't know.

Dee was jolted out of her fog by a flashing yellow apparition headed straight toward her. Jack O'Reilly usually ran with his two German Shepherds, but today all he had were his battery-operated blinkers and a new phosphorescent orange stripe down each side of his shorts. Dee released her grip on her pepper spray and nodded at Jack as they passed.

As she went by Morty's Meat Market, she slowed, knowing that her turn-around point was near. She reached the street corner and shuffled in place, waiting for the cross traffic to pass. Her anger at her friends only increased her irritation at having to wait at the corner.

As usual, there were few cars about. After a van with peeling brown paint ground through its gears as it chugged across the intersection, the only vehicle left was a black motorcycle which sat idling at the corner. The rider waved Dee across.

Tired of treading the same square of sidewalk, Dee took advantage of the generous offer. Her thoughts returned to the mysteries of relationships as she sprung off the curb. At that moment, the low growl of the motorcycle revved to high. It leapt towards her.

Shocked into reality, Dee sprinted. The motorcycle ripped onward. She glanced at the gleaming bike. The driver held something long in a black-gloved hand.

The wheels of the cycle clipped Dee's heels. She dove for the sidewalk, digging in her pocket for her pepper spray. She felt the jagged surface of the asphalt tear into her knees as she skidded. She pressed the spray button as the driver's left arm swung upwards.

A heavy wooden object crashed towards her, her last vision of the morning.

Dee could hear familiar voices around her. Given that these were voices of the living, she knew she wasn't dead. The pounding of her head made her wonder if life was the preferable state.

Between cranial throbs, Dee began to attach names to voices. The Texas drawl that was Tully. The huskiness of Quinn. The baritone of Pierce. The lilting low of Evie.

Evie? The thought almost caused Dee's eyes to fly open. Almost. The light already coming through her closed lids made the thought of opening them unappealing.

Through Dee's haze she caught snips and snatches of the conversation. Jack O'Reilly. Motorcycle. Unknown driver. Blunt object.

"Bat," Dee said, eyes firmly shut.

The silence that fell made her aware her words had been heard.

She tried again. "Not blunt. Bat. Baseball bat." Exhausted, she sunk back into the twilight world of semi-consciousness.

When Dee re-awoke, it was to a distant hum of activity. No conversation. No bright lights.

With trepidation she opened her eyelids. No blur. Just the sight of Evie in what Dee referred to as her therapist pose:

upright, hands clasped in her lap, legs crossed at the knee, eyes looking straight ahead. Instead of being intent upon a client, Evie seemed to be focused on the scene outside the window. A frown creased her brow.

Dee tried her voice. "Hey there."

"Hey there, back." Evie shifted in her chair to face Dee. A slight smile moved the lines from her forehead to her dimples. She rose and stood beside Dee's bed. Reaching out, she stroked Dee's chin. "How's the head?"

Up until then Dee hadn't been conscious of any nerve impulses from that region. Directing her attention to her head she realized the pounding was gone and only an ache and tightness remained.

"Actually, I feel OK. A lot better than before." Dee leaned on one elbow to hoist herself up, but Evie's hand on her shoulder stopped her.

"Don't even think about it, hotshot. I rang for the doctor. Wait 'til he sees you. Then we'll know what's what."

Dee sank back onto the firm bed. "Was that Tully and the good detectives I heard earlier?"

"You really were awake. We didn't know if your comment was from a dream or if you were contributing to the conversation." Evie sat gently on the edge of the bed. "So you heard the other jogger found you and called an ambulance?"

"I gathered. And Jack must have seen the motorcycle."

Evie nodded. "But he couldn't give a description of it or the driver. Can you?"

"An excellent question, Ms. Taylor." Gina Quinn's smoky voice caused both Evie and Dee to turn towards the door.

In Dee's case, the abrupt movement was a mistake. The ache became a blinding flash. Her eyes slammed shut. She moaned.

The doctor must have accompanied Detective Quinn into the room. Within seconds the space was cleared and Dee was subjected to the poking and prodding which gave the medical profession such a good name.

The doctor grunted and left. Dee could hear faint voices in the hallway as she gathered herself to sit in a more vertical direction. Pleased to find she could raise herself to more dizzying heights without the dizzy part, Dee ran her fingers through her disheveled hair.

Her fingers encountered bandages. She probed the large one on her right side and was sorry. Stealing herself, she touched the smaller patch on the left. It was sore, but not nearly so swollen. Dee shut her eyes and tried to replay the scene with the motorcycle. Before she could bring forth the memory, Tully's voice recalled her to the room.

"Howdy, good buddy." Tully smiled down at her, but worry filled her eyes. "The doc says you're doing fine. Do you want to rest for a while?"

Dee refrained from shaking her head. "No, I was just trying to figure out what happened."

"Evie said you remember some of it."

"Sure. The guy on the motorcycle and that baseball bat flying out of the air. After that, not much."

"Think you can help our pals Gina and Alex with some descriptions?"

"Gina? And Alex?" Dee could not keep the amazement from her voice. "Are we still in Kansas, Toto? How long have I been out? How did I miss the exchange of first names?"

"Glad to see your sense of humor is intact." Tully settled her long frame in the chair beside Dee's bed. "We've been having a little powwow while you've been napping. The detective duo weren't exactly enamored with our manuscript scheme."

"It was a stupid move." Pierce's voice broke their tete-a-tete. "Unless you set this whole thing up to try to turn suspicion away from yourself."

"Untrusting soul, aren't you?" Dee pulled the covers over her chest at the sight of the sandy-haired detective. "Sorry, but I have much too low a pain threshold to deliberately do myself bodily harm."

Pierce's face remained a blank.

"I take it you didn't get the license plate of that Yamaha?" Dee asked.

Pierce flipped open his worn leather notebook. "Is that the model of the motorcycle?"

"You bet. I owned one for five years before I took off two layers of skin and a lot of dignity in an accident on Lankershim. It was a Yamaha 550, black, at least two years old. They changed the position of the headlight a few years ago."

Pierce wrote quickly then looked up. "What about the driver?"

Dee started to swing her head. The pain alerted her to the stupidity of that particular move. She waved Pierce and Tully back with one hand as she cradled her forehead with the other. The room stopped swimming.

"I didn't get a good look at him. He was wearing dark clothes, dark jacket, and a tinted visor on his helmet."

"You keep saying 'him', Ms. DelValle. Could it have been a woman?"

Dee looked at Pierce with new respect. "How liberal of you— and how sexist of me." She thought about the size and shape of the driver's body. "It's hard to judge when a person's sitting on a bike, all bent over. But it could have been a woman. I know a lot of women who can ride as well as this Bozo did and can swing a bat a whole lot better."

"Which arm did he or she use?"

Dee did not hesitate. "Left."

Pierce nodded and rubbed his jaw. Dee noted it had the beginnings of a five o'clock shadow. She didn't know if that was a clue to the time of day or a testimony to the hectic nature of the detective's schedule.

"Is that important?"

"It's just that Ms. Shelbourne's attacker was probably left handed." Pierce straightened and flipped his notebook closed. "If you can think of any additional details, we'd appreciate the help. Frankly, this is turning out to be a mare's nest of a case."

"What do you mean?" Dee looked from Tully to Pierce and watched the two exchange a glance. "What's going on?"

Tully reached over and covered Dee's hand with hers. "While you were out, a new wrinkle developed."

"What happened? Has anybody else been hurt?"

Tully flicked a look at Pierce then squeezed Dee's hands. "Your neighbor, Amy Holmes, called. Somebody ransacked your house."

Chapter 16

"Maybe it's time to redecorate."

Tully's observation did not distract Dee from the disaster that used to be her living room. She reached for a blue ceramic vase which lay on the carpet and cradled it for a moment. Then she replaced it on her mantelpiece, despite the chip on its lip and the crack along one side.

Dee stepped over a dozen books to reach one on California history which her mother had given her last Christmas. The pages were bent and the spine wrinkled, but the binding was still intact. She dusted off one shelf on the wrought iron bookcase and replaced the lone book.

The headache, which had abated overnight at the hospital, threatened to reemerge bigger and stronger than ever.

Stepping around and over the piles of magazines and books on the floor, Dee struggled toward her office with Tully silently following in her wake. From the doorway Dee could see the remains of her sanctuary.

Where bright weavings and woven blankets had once covered the walls, bare paint glared. The low bookshelves that ringed the room were empty, their contents strewn upon the ground. Art supplies had occupied a closet that Dee had personally converted into an open cabinet. Now the paints, clay, pencils, and canvas just added to the debris on the floor.

Dee's jaw grew even tighter when she noticed her new Macintosh computer. Parts of it were sticking out from under the rest of the rubble on the carpet. She bent down and brushed aside the torn weavings to uncover the machine, its smashed screen forlorn. She picked up the keyboard and swung around to face Tully. The fury she felt must have been reflected in her eyes for Tully's face filled with concern.

"I know what you're thinking, good buddy, but I'm not sure killing this jerk is the best idea. After all, I thought the whole idea was to keep you out of jail."

Dee glared. "You want me to be a punching bag? You think I should turn the other cheek?"

"Nope. Never had much use for doormats and I can't see you turning into one either." Tully kicked a chart out of her way and stepped over to Dee. She waved at the room. "You know what all this means, don't you? It means he's the one who's scared. He wants that manuscript and he thinks you've got it. I'll bet he wet his pants when he couldn't find it anywhere."

Dee retrieved one of her paintbrushes, its horsehair bristles splayed. She twirled it in her hands. "Or maybe he realized the manuscript doesn't exist."

Tully mulled that thought for a moment. "He can't risk that. He's got to figure you really do have it, but that you don't know the value of what you have. So he's got to get to it before you wise up and start flashing it around to all the wrong people, like, say, the police."

"You realize that scenario means that whacking me on the head and trashing my house won't be enough for him next time?"

"We'll make sure there is no next time." Tully wrapped an arm around Dee's shoulder. "We're going to find the bastard and we're going to do it now."

Tully and Felicia propped pillows under Dee's legs and brought her iced tea and peanut butter cookies, her second favorite kind. Anger at her attacker still blazed within her, but it didn't prevent her from relaxing on Felicia's couch. She enjoyed the peanut butter melting on her tongue even while feeling the rage.

Dee gazed out the front window which framed the hillside of Mount Washington. Felicia's house was down-home country with lots of blues and cotton and brass fixtures. As Dee melted into a mixture of indignation and indulgence, her thoughts returned to her home. The rumination created an unexpected ache in her heart.

She decided she would donate most of her things to Out of the Closet. The charity would come and take away all the furniture that wasn't nailed down. She'd have to sort through all the damage to rescue keepsakes, but she wasn't willing to live with reminders of the violation, which meant changes needed to be made.

"Hey, Felicia!" Dee called. "How would you like to help me fix up my house?"

Felicia poked her head around the corner from the kitchen. "Now, girlfriend, you know there's nothing I like better than chasing around garage sales and flea markets. That's just not your style."

"Not true. I think I want to try a more homey feel."

Felicia came through the doorway and put her hand to Dee's forehead. "Honey, is your head acting up again?"

Dee slapped Felicia's hand away. "Don't you start."

Tully marched into the room with Dee's chart and easel in hand. "Good thing I had this at my house or our perp would know all that we know. Which, to some cynics, might not look like a lot. But that would be untrue."

She angled the equipment so that the ample sunlight from the window fell on the large pad of paper. She then clomped one booted foot on the side table and leaned towards the chart. "As you all can see, Plan One was a great success. We got the killer's attention. And, as a bonus, our good detective friends are not quite so sure they are on the right track anymore."

Dee perked up. "Is this inside information or a hunch?"

Tully waggled her eyebrows. "Discretion forbids I say more."

Felicia snorted. "The ice maiden was still frozen last time I looked."

Disregarding Felicia, Tully pointed to the chart. "As assigned, I checked into Sheila's father. Mr. Shelbourne, does, indeed, have a history of violence. At least there was one police call regarding domestic violence."

"He beat up his wife? How in the world did you ever find that out? It couldn't have been through Ms. Detective." Felicia eased herself down on the couch beside Dee.

"No, Gina didn't have anything to do with that."

At Tully's use of the detective's first name Dee and Felicia looked at each other and rolled their eyes in unison.

Ignoring them, Tully continued, "Do you remember Cheryl? The really cute brunette I met on the Olivia Cruise to Hawaii?"

"Oh, yeah." Felicia laid her head on Dee's lap. "Didn't she last longer than usual?"

"She sure did," Dee agreed, stroking Felicia's tight curls. "At least three weeks. A record at the time."

"If you're through?" Tully drew herself to her full height, crossed her arms, and resumed. "I called Cheryl because she just happens to work in the Records Department at City Hall and she knows how to access the Police Department's files."

Felicia sniffed. "She wouldn't have done that. Releasing that kind of information would cost her her job."

"What information did she release? All she did was tell me the date that police might have been called to that street and suggested I check for newspaper accounts."

Dee winced. Tully was neither immoral nor amoral, though she sometimes skirted the line. Dee worried when that happened. She also worried about the part she was playing in tempting her buddy to dip her toes into illegal waters. "Tully, I'd hate to get out of a jail sentence by having you serve one instead."

"Would I do that?" Tully tried her best to look innocent. But when you're blessed with bedroom eyes and full, sensuous lips, innocence is not an easy look to achieve. "It seems there was a violent altercation between two males, names not given since the one on the receiving end did not file charges. Anyway, I haven't gotten to the best part."

"More vague innuendoes?" Felicia remained reclined as she reached for a cookie. She passed the plate to Dee as Tully continued.

"Since I was there, I looked at the Los Angeles Times and the San Diego Newspress libraries for the last twenty years. I checked on any other news stories about Sheila or her family. It seems Sheila had a sister, Natalie."

"I never knew she had a sister," Dee said. "But what does this Natalie have to do with Sheila's murder?"

"Sister Natalie committed suicide about ten years back. And one Harry Shelbourne, also known as Dear Old Dad, was questioned but released. It seems Natalie's suicide occurred under what were described as suspicious circumstances."

Chapter 17

"Get the hell out of my house!" Henry Shelbourne glared at the two women in front of him.

This was not at all the same reception with which Mr. Shelbourne had originally greeted Dee and Tully. When they first rang his doorbell, Shelbourne had welcomed them in with a reserved smile. His eyes were shielded behind steel rimmed glasses, his graying brown hair fluffed out to try to hide the thinness around the temples.

Seeing this man who had just lost his daughter, Dee felt guilty about obtaining an interview using the pretext of their mythical copy of Sheila's manuscript. She would have felt guiltier if she and Tully had not spotted a motorcycle covered with a tarp parked beside the Shelbourne's garage. The one fender that peeked out from under the cover was black.

Dee had decided that a direct approach was the best on this matter. Before Mr. Shelbourne could even usher them inside, she had motioned to the tarped vehicle. "Looks like a nice bike there. Is it a Yamaha?"

Mr. Shelbourne shrugged his slim shoulders. "I'm afraid I haven't the faintest. Steve, Sheila's husband, asked if he could park it here. He mentioned something about not having room in his garage and it being unsafe to park it on the street in his neighborhood."

Conversation had turned to their relationship to Sheila, a recitation that was carefully edited. Then he asked about

Sheila's book. It was their suggestion that he had engineered his first daughter's death that provoked his hostility.

"I don't have to listen to any of this slander." Shelbourne slammed his fist on the arm of his chair and stepped to the fireplace. "Get out of here!"

Dee didn't even look at Tully who was ensconced on the love seat. She just leaned back into the couch of the glacial living room. Shelbourne's outburst only deepened her suspicions about him. "Natalie died because of you. Did Sheila?"

Shelbourne's wiry frame had not seemed menacing when they had arrived. Now it seemed to Dee that his bulk had doubled. His eyes blazed at her as he stood by the white marble fireplace. Dee's gaze flicked to the brass-handled poker and shovel which leaned inches from his hand.

Shelbourne gripped the edge of the mantelpiece. "I don't have to listen to your filthy allegations."

"They're not mine. They're Sheila's."

"That's a lie." Shelbourne started toward her, hands forming fists. "Sheila would never dare write that about me. Why would she ever say that?"

Dee stood and faced him. She met and held Shelbourne's glare. Into the deathly quiet of the room, she took her shot in the dark. "Abuse."

Shelbourne barked a laugh. "That's ridiculous. Just a bunch of psychological hogwash therapists invented to keep themselves in business. In my day, parents were expected to set high standards for their children. If more people did that nowadays, we'd have a lot fewer problems in the world."

Dee shook her head. "Sheila didn't see it that way. She blamed you for Natalie's death."

"No she didn't. It was that therapist of hers who put those thoughts in her head. Sheila whined about me because she needed to blame someone for her life. Look at her! She couldn't hold a good man when she had him. She settled for a little local newscaster job. She was a doormat, not a fighter." He banged a side table causing framed photos to slide. "If she had any guts, she would have been a national prime time newscaster by now."

"Was Natalie a doormat, too?"

Shelbourne's face twitched. "Natalie." He leaned forward, bracing himself on the back of the overstuffed armchair. "That girl was a loser from the time she was born. She never could do anything right. She picked out loser boyfriends and couldn't even make the grades for a decent grad school."

"So both your daughters disappointed you. I guess their deaths were no loss for you. Maybe they were even a relief."

Shelbourne took a step towards Dee. "How dare you suggest that!"

With Mr. Shelbourne's sudden advance, Dee looked over to Tully for ideas, but Tully was not in the love seat. Instead, Dee spotted her standing behind Henry Shelbourne, fireplace shovel raised over her shoulder in a tense grip, her eyes focused on Shelbourne's bald spot.

"Tully!"

Dee's shout caused Shelbourne to swing around. At the sight of Tully towering over him like an avenging angel with an iron sword, he blanched.

Tully lowered the shovel to her shoulder. "Just trying to even the odds in case our Mr. Nice Guy here decided to do more than threaten."

Shelbourne kept an eye on Tully as he backed as far away as he could. Once out of reach, he said, "I think you should leave now before I call the police."

Tully shrugged. "Why don't you? Then we can all sit around and have a nice chat with the homicide detectives. Maybe they'd be interested in Sheila's thoughts."

"I had this discussion with the police many years ago. I doubt they'll be any more interested now than they were then."

Dee removed the shovel from Tully's fist, replaced it on the hearth, and led the way out of the house.

"Jessica Fletcher couldn't have done any better," Tully said as the two women drove out of the Palisades.

Dee disagreed. "Jessica Fletcher would have not only found out where Mr. Shelbourne was on that fatal night, but would have tripped him up on some technicality that only the murderer could have known."

"Jessica had a finished script. We're still trying to write ours."

Dee settled back into the warm purple corduroy of the passenger's seat of her car. She tried to keep her head still as Tully slid the sedan around the bends of Sunset Boulevard. Tully had to take the curves more slowly than she would have with her Jeep. But the Hyundai only mitigated Tully's aggressive driving style a tiny bit.

Dee, Tully, and Felicia had argued over Dee driving herself to the Shelbourne's. Dee had wanted to tackle Mr. Shelbourne by herself. Outnumbered, she allowed herself to be chauffeured in deference to her concussion.

"How did you come up with that zinger about abuse?" Tully asked. "I thought I'd drop my teeth on that one."

Dee shrugged. "That was Evie's guess, not mine. What did you make of his response?"

"Well Father Knows Best, he's not. I sure wouldn't want to grow up under that dude's standards." Tully frowned. "And there's that little fact of the motorcycle. Do we believe it belongs to Stunning Steve, or was Daddy Dear throwing suspicion in his direction?"

"That doesn't seem to fit Steve's glowing report of his relationship with Sheila's folks."

"Maybe Steve is the bad guy." Tully started to bounce in the driver's seat. "That's it. It wasn't a therapist who did it. It was Steve who poisoned Sheila's feeble brain against her own father so that Sheila would disinherit her family. Then when Sheila realized the truth, she confronted Steve and he killed her."

"That might work if Sheila had any money, and if Sheila

were still married to Steve, and if Steve still gave a hoot about how Sheila and her dad were getting along, and if…"

"Whoa little doggies." Tully cut her off. "I hear you don't like my scenario. But what about money? Who did get Sheila's dough? Could Dear Old Dad need the money and clonked his daughter to get some? Maybe he found out she was making a new will that excluded him because she did blame him for being an abusive ass or for her sister's death or…"

"Whoa your own horse. Did you just jump from Steve to Dad as chief suspect?"

Tully shook her head in mock dismay. "Steeplechasers jump. I ride in dignity wherever the trail leads."

"Even when that's over the edge of a cliff. "

Chapter 18

Dee chewed her lower lip. "So what do we do now?" She stood in Felicia's living room considering the chart of suspects and alibis. The three women had argued over where to put the information about the black motorcycle. They compromised on listing it under both Steve and the Shelbournes with a question mark beside it.

"No way to the honey without sticking your hand in the hive."

Dee and Tully both turned to Felicia with expectant looks upon their faces.

"For you city folk, it means the only way to find out what we need to know is to go talk to the devil in person." She sat up. "That's how I found out about our station manager, Curtis, and his disappearing act."

"Disappearing act?" Dee asked.

"Sure enough. Remember the assistant director couldn't find Curtis the night Sheila was killed? It seems the A.D. never found him and when I mentioned that to Curtis, he told me he had a meeting about a potential commercial account."

Dee stood and walked to the chart. She grabbed a blue pen to fill in Curtis' whereabouts as a single witness piece of information then stopped. "Did anyone else see Curtis go to this meeting?"

"Nope. Nobody saw him leave or come back. I should check with Gloria, his secretary, to see if she knew anything about the appointment." Felicia grabbed a piece of paper to write herself a note.

Dee faced the chart and pondered what color to use. She contemplated using yellow for an unsubstantiated alibi so that if it were later given credence, she could darken it in. But the untidiness of adding another color to the chart convinced her to stick with her original idea of blue. She was mollified by the thought that she could underline it in red if it were later collaborated.

She stepped back and studied her multicolored creation. If they limited themselves to considering the suspects who had access to a black BMW, then they needed to zero in on Henry and Amanda Shelbourne, Rachel O'Neil, the now found-to-be-missing Curtis Lee, and Sheila's ex, Steve Montgomery. Dee's eyes were drawn back to the list of cars and she felt her blood leave her face.

"Oh my gosh, I totally forgot."

Felicia and Tully turned away from a squabble over the last remaining peanut butter cookie to focus on Dee.

Dee picked up a black pen, then reconsidered and grabbed a blue for single witness. She wrote on the paper as she spoke. "I went to see Jenny. She was at Sheila's condo soon after I left. She claims she found Sheila dead."

Felicia's gasp made Dee swing around to face her. Seeing the shock on Felicia's face convinced Dee that she wasn't alone in being left in the dark about Jenny's activities. Dee filled Felicia in on Jenny's story, all the while noting that Tully did not seem surprised at any of the information.

"So," Dee concluded, "unless we want to include Jenny in our list of suspects, we've got to assume the killer was in Sheila's condo when I was at her door and that he or she left between Jenny's arrival and my departure."

Felicia's jaw had hung open at the beginning of Dee's tale. At the suggestion that Jenny might be a suspect, it snapped shut. "No way did Jenny have anything to do with that woman's death. To even think that is…" She stuttered to a stop.

"Disloyal?" Dee swiveled her eyes to Tully. "It's really awful to think that a friend knew something like this and didn't tell you."

Tully opened her mouth then closed it. She looked down at her folded fists and sighed. "I didn't know Jenny had gone to see Sheila, but I did know about their affair." She stared hard at Dee. "I also knew how that blonde bimbo treated Jenny and that's why I was ready to hog-tie you when you started sniffing after that tart, especially when you had such a fine woman as Evie already on your hands."

"Would have been nice if you'd told me."

"It's Jenny's story to tell, not mine."

Felicia broke in with a bewildered voice. "How do you know all this? And why is Jenny worried about Sheila including her in the book?"

Tully sighed again. "There's more to the story than Jenny let you know, but I can't tell you without her permission."

Dee clinched her jaw. "Then I think it's time for Jenny to share with us all."

"I think the Reader's Digest version may be best."

Jenny reigned over her living room. She sat, erect, once again on the Swedish modern chair by the fireplace while Dee, Tully, and Felicia huddled on the couch. The late afternoon sun lit the left side of her angular face. Dee could see a deepening of the fine lines branching from Jenny's eyes. This was the only sign of stress that Dee could detect on her friend's face.

At Dee's insistence, Tully had arranged this meeting. It had been Dee's hope to not only clear up the mystery of Jenny and Sheila's relationship, but to also shed light on the murder. Now, sensing Jenny's coldness, Tully's annoyance, and Felicia's confusion, Dee felt her hopes shrinking like Alice disappearing down the rabbit hole.

Dee cleared her throat and floated a trial grin. "Will the condensed version be hard to follow? I'm not sure about my mental agility at the moment." Her grin slid off her face as the rest of the ensemble failed to reflect the easing of any tension.

Jenny looked directly at Dee. "I never intended for any of this to come to light. Only a few people know. A few very trusted souls." With this, Jenny shifted her gaze to Tully and their eyes locked with a tenderness that was almost palpable.

Dee sucked in her breath. Was it possible that Tully and Jenny...? She shot a glance at Felicia who also seemed mesmerized by the scene. Dee felt like the baseball bat had just hit her over the head again. Dazed and confused, she broke into everyone's reverie. "Before I go jumping to any, hopefully wrong, conclusions here, why don't you let the rest of us in on all this?"

"All right, I'll give you the whole fairy tale. But you'll have to indulge me as I recount a little history." Jenny leaned back, her long, thick fingers playing with the seam of the leather chair arm. She closed her eyes. "Once upon a time in a small town outside of Houston, there lived a young man named Kenneth James, but his friends called him Jimmy. This, by the way, infuriated his father, Kenneth Senior, but such is the way of life.

"Jimmy grew up and went away to college, as far away as his own earnings could take him from his family. There he met a wonderful woman. Actually, he met several wonderful women, but this particular tale has nothing to do with them." As Jenny proceeded with her tale, Dee noticed a drawl creeping into Jenny's usual California flat accent.

"To continue, Jimmy met a tall, sexy blonde with the unusual name of Tallulah." Dee and Felicia turned simultaneously to stare at Tully who did not return their interest. She was smiling gently at Jenny.

"The two began a rather wild love affair that quickly turned more to friendship than romance. This, in itself, was unusual, for to the outside observer these two had little in common. Jimmy was dirt poor, undereducated, and knew only his hometown and the city of Houston. Tallulah was exceedingly rich, thanks to her dear old daddy's computer chip invention, and had been schooled throughout the world. However, friends they became, and it was to Jimmy that Tallulah first admitted her attraction to other women."

"Goodness gracious, girl. You mean you went and told some hetero hunk before you let your sisters around you know?" Felicia had her hands on her hips, although Dee wasn't sure how she could manage that particular physical maneuver while surrounded by the softness of the sofa's cushions.

Tully reached out and squeezed Felicia's arm. "There were extenuating circumstances."

Dee shook her head. "So what does all this have to do with anything?"

Jenny broke in. "When the time is right, all will be made clear to you. At least that's what the Mormon elders used to tell us when we questioned some of the more esoteric tenets of the Church."

"You're Mormon?" This time it was Felicia who interrupted.

"Jack Mormon. But that's another story for another evening." Jenny leaned back again and resumed. "As I was saying, Tallulah made known her interest in the same sex. It was Jimmy who supported her decision to explore her new lifestyle and who provided her with a cover. In those days it was still pretty taboo to be gay, even in Houston.

"Despite Tallulah's example of bravery, Jimmy kept a part of himself hidden, the part that had driven him away from his family and away from his Church. Jimmy, who was known far and wide on campus as a great stud, hated being a man."

Chapter 19

Silence descended on the little group. Dee's head spun as the ramifications of Jenny's statement became manifest.

Twilight filtered through the windows and Jenny's face was washed by shadows as she picked up the thread. "Now Jimmy, lacking funds and courage, had never done anything about his predicament. Plus, he had this confusing complication. You see, although he knew that deep inside he wasn't really a he, he also knew he loved women. And he didn't see this ever changing. So what did that make him? One very confused and lonely individual.

"Jimmy decided to end it all. He hated blood and the thought of shooting himself brought back memories of his dad trying to teach him to hunt jack rabbits. His failings in that arena only intensified his dad's disappointment in Jimmy as a real man."

The chair creaked as Jenny leaned further back, her face hidden from the light. "Jimmy couldn't shoot himself, so he tried the overdose route. He manfully downed forty or fifty pain pills with a six-pack of beer. Tallulah found him, saved his life, and finally dragged the entire story from him." Jenny sighed and shifted yet again. "Tallulah, being the intelligent, resourceful individual that she is, not only got Jimmy the psychological counseling he needed, but, when the time came, she paid for Jimmy's hormone therapy and his series of operations."

Jenny sat up straight, eyes blinking back tears which

sparkled in the early evening light. She faced Tully. "You gave me my life. Sheila was trying to take it all away."

"But how did Sheila find out?" Felicia's bewilderment was evident.

Jenny smiled gently. "She could tell right away when we went to bed together. Some things are rather obvious."

Their gaze met momentarily. Then Felicia sank back on the couch and looked away.

"That's no reason to kill her." Dee's voice sounded harsh even to her own ears.

"I didn't."

"But, you just said…"

Jenny shook her head. "I said Sheila was trying to destroy the life I had made for myself. She was threatening to expose me as transgender. Of course, she didn't think of it as a threat. She actually called me to tell me that she had included me in her autobiography. She honestly thought I'd be honored." Jenny's eyes grew hard. "That self-centered cow had no clue what that would do to me, my career, my friendships, even my family back in Taylorville, Texas who think I've just disappeared off the face of the Earth."

Dee had a sudden inspiration. "When did she call?"

"Thursday night." Jenny's voice now sounded weary.

Dee felt smug having her deduction validated. She was beginning to suspect that Sheila's telephone bill from that night might be huge, and very informative. Unfortunately, she could think of no means of obtaining it.

She also wondered about the book. Unfinished, it would be no threat since it wouldn't be published and no one would ever learn Sheila's version of her life. If she had finished it, but not submitted it, then her parents would probably have the rights to it. Thinking of Henry Shelbourne, Dee doubted the manuscript would ever see the light of day if that were the case. On the other hand, if she had finished it, and if a publisher had agreed to print it, it gave Sheila's invitation to Dee a different meaning. Maybe Sheila was celebrating having her book accepted.

"Did Sheila say she had finished her book or that she was still writing it?" Dee asked.

"Good point, good buddy. If she wasn't finished there would be no reason for anyone to steal it or worry about it. But if she had…" Tully drifted off in thought.

Jenny looked at the other two quizzically, obviously not following their change of focus. "I don't know. I was so upset that I don't think I registered everything she said. I was so angry that she would do that to me after using me and dumping me, I just couldn't think."

Dee stretched out her legs and stared down the length of her twenty-seven inch inseamed jeans. She waited for the others to ask the hard questions, but the shadows drifting over the hardwood floors made more noise than either Tully or Felicia.

She leaned into the corner of the couch. She wanted to believe Jenny was innocent, but her motive seemed so strong.

Dee suddenly felt very alone.

She breached the void. "So why did you go to Sheila's condo last Friday?"

"I told you," Jenny said with a sigh. "I didn't want her to put me in that book. Not by name, not by innuendo, not by any means at all."

"But why did you wait until Friday? Why not Thursday night?"

"It was late when she called. I had an early morning news conference set for Friday. I thought it would wait. I thought I should calm down." Jenny chewed the lipstick off her bottom lip. "If I had gone there that night, I really might have killed her."

On that score, Dee believed her. She was also aware that it got them no nearer the truth. "So you never got to talk with Sheila. You didn't see anybody in her home. There's nothing you can tell me that will help at all." Dee didn't bother to keep the frustration out of her voice.

Jenny held up a finger. "Actually, there is one thing. When I first drove up and saw your Hyundai, I sat in my car for a few minutes trying to decide what to do. That was when I noticed this really big guy walking back and forth in front of Sheila's building. I only remember him because he was wearing a Seville suit and a homburg. He looked like an ad for 'GQ'."

Dee nodded. "I think I know who you mean. I saw him there before I went in."

"Tully was filling me in on some of your findings. When she mentioned Lurch, I remembered him from the wake. At the time I thought he looked familiar, but he wasn't wearing a hat then, so I didn't piece it together."

Dee and Felicia looked at each other. Dee thumped the upholstery. "Stunning Steve Montgomery."

Felicia grinned. "And his hat."

Chapter 20

Dee feared she might be sticking more than her hand into the hive. She had called Steve Montgomery to suggest a cup of coffee and he had countered with first meeting at his place. She could see no easy way to invent an excuse, not if she were going to kick start this investigation on her own. She needed to find out if the motorcycle really belonged to him or if Mr. Shelbourne was throwing out a red herring. She also wanted to know if he had indeed gone to see his ex-wife on the evening of her death. She had too many questions to be squeamish about where the interview took place.

The drive to North Hollywood flew by faster than Dee's busy mind would have liked. She arrived at the sedate, wood-sided two-story apartment building with enough time to spare to allow her nerves to rev into high gear. She carefully locked the door of her Hyundai as she surveyed the street.

Steve's building was a '50s style complex with a landscaped center courtyard. Two rows of facing doorways opened onto the garden. This rather cozy structure was set off by slick, three-story, stucco apartment buildings on either side. If she had to choose, Dee agreed with Steve's nod towards character over modernization.

She rapped on his front door right on time. The door swung partway open under her knuckles, but Steve was not visible in the opening.

"Steve?" Dee hesitated before pushing the door open.

Relationships Can Be Murder

Despite her head replaying every horror film she had ever seen, Dee edged the door open with the back of her knuckles. Her ears were alert for any hint of sound.

"Steve?" she called again as she slid into his living room. Still no response.

Now standing in the living room, she paused to let her eyes adjust to the darkness. The drapes on the front picture window were closed, muting the strong morning sun. The light from the open door allowed Dee to discern a long upholstered couch and a matching wing back chair grouped around a wooden spool coffee table. She crept further into the room, holding her breath as she neared the couch. It was empty, as were the chair and the carpeted floor of the room.

Relaxing her shoulders a bit, she cast around for any signs of occupancy. No newspapers or mail littered the tabletop; no clothing was strewn on the furniture. Her nose picked up the faint scent of flowers, but no bouquet was in evidence.

Dee considered her options. The honorable thing to do was to leave, locking and shutting the door behind her. Maybe she could even contact Steve's apartment manager and report Steve's open door. Of course, if she did that she'd miss out on the chance to find out something about one of her best suspects. This whole moral debate continued to rage in her mind even as she found herself peeking under the cushions of his couch and sliding pictures to see if they covered a wall safe.

Dee noticed several envelopes in a wooden box beside the telephone. The answering machine had no messages showing, but there was a small pad of paper and a pen beside it. Several notations were scribbled on the top sheet. Dee read through them: George—SD leave extend? Curt—x508, H.S.—dinner, D— 10 coffee. Using a Kleenex to cover her fingers, she hurriedly flipped through the opened mail in the box. All were bills or other impersonal missives addressed to Steven Montgomery except for one. The return address was from an apartment or condo on San Gregorio Drive in Brentwood.

Dee opened the envelope only to discover it was empty. She was sifting through the pad of paper hoping to find the missing letter when she heard footsteps approaching Steve's front door. She threw the pad back on the desk and scrambled around the coffee table to position herself in front of a large abstract oil painting. Placing her hands behind her back, she assumed what she hoped was an air of innocence as she listened to the footsteps near, and then pass, Steve's entry. The slapping of tennis shoes continued up the stairs and soon a door slammed overhead.

Deciding not to waste any more time, she entered a short hall. To the left seemed to be the bedroom and bath. To the right was the kitchen. The kitchen seemed a safer bet.

Steve, she decided, was an abnormal male. Most single straight men she knew lived, to put it charitably, like pigs. Steve's kitchen would make Martha Stewart proud. The sink, counters, and floor sparkled. The dish towels were clean and neatly hung. She resisted the temptation to look into his refrigerator, although she fantasized that it would be spotless with matching containers all neatly labeled with the contents and the date. A man after her own heart.

Dee smiled at the thought, then sobered as she realized she was only delaying her foray into the rest of the apartment.

Deciding to leave the bathroom for last, Dee crept towards what she could only assume to be the bedroom. Her conscience had lost the wrestling match over her snooping. Somehow a little judicious peering about now seemed not only a good and right course of action, but morally superior to just waiting for others to do all the investigating.

The bedroom was guarded by a pocket door that was pulled out about five inches from the frame. Dee knocked on this slight bit of pine and called Steve's name yet again. When silence was once more the familiar response, she poked her head inside the partially opened doorway.

Dee immediately wished she hadn't.

All the books she had ever read, all the movies she had ever seen, all of them had the luckless discoverers of dead bodies check for a pulse.

The only body Dee wanted to check for signs of life was her own.

She leaned against the doorway shutting her eyes to the ramshackled room and Steve Montgomery's bloodied corpse.

Dee fought down panic and straightened her spine against the door frame. Then, remembering the telephone, she started down the hall towards the living room. A gun greeted her.

The fact that the gun was in the hands of a six foot man with a glare in his dark eyes didn't help Dee feel any better.

"Freeze. Put your hands up."

Before Dee could point out to him that these were contradictory orders, another armed person joined Tall Dark Man. Only then did the uniforms of the LAPD make any impression on her.

Without lowering his gun, Tall Dark asked, "Who are you? What are you doing here?"

The police interrogation room, Dee reflected wryly, was beginning to seem like home. Another visit here and she'd ask if she could hang a few pictures to liven up the place.

She wasn't sure whether to bless or curse Steve's upstairs neighbor who had called the police over the noise of destruction downstairs. The close timing of her arrival and the call to the police led Dee to conclude that the murder happened just before she knocked on his door.

The more she mulled over her innocent explanation of events, the more convinced she became of her own guilt. She supposed that had something to do with her Catholic upbringing. She only hoped Quinn and Pierce didn't share her religious background.

Gina Quinn slammed open the metal door. Pierce didn't look any happier as he followed his partner into the room. Dee sud-

Jane DiLucchio					*123*

denly realized she had a major craving for a piece of Boston cream pie.

Knowing food was not forthcoming, Dee straightened her back and took the offensive. "Did you know Steve Montgomery visited his ex-wife the night of her death? And that he owns a black motorcycle?"

"What were you doing at his apartment?" Quinn's hand slapped the table as she slid into a chair.

Dee frowned down at Quinn's left hand and noted a lighter shade of olive below the knuckle of the now bare third finger. Filing away that tidbit of information, Dee gave a brief run down of her plans to meet Steve and have coffee.

"You called a man for a date? A man who you suspected attacked you and murdered your lover?" Quinn's face reflected all the disbelief that was absent from her voice.

"I know it sounds fishy."

"You wouldn't have been trying to play detective, now would you?" Pierce sounded mellow rather than sarcastic.

Dee had a sudden inspiration. "I just wanted to check out the facts before coming to you. I didn't want to waste your time with unsubstantiated rumors."

Pierce and Quinn didn't seem to share her view of herself as a conscientious citizen. They both shook their heads before Gina Quinn asked, "Are there any other unsubstantiated rumors you've heard that you'd like to share?"

"A few." Dee filled them in on Mr. Shelbourne and the presumed abuse of his daughters as well as Curtis Lee's disappearance and the presence of the black BMWs on Sheila's street. Jenny and her discoveries were missing from this recitation of facts, hearsay, and supposition.

Dee concluded, "I don't suppose you know where everyone was when Sheila was killed?"

"Ms. DelValle, we are not in the position to share anything with you. This is a one-way exchange only." Quinn stood and whacked her notebook against one twill-encased leg. "You should, by rights, be in jail. Two murders and you, conveniently, on hand for both."

Dee's nervousness, stress, and fear morphed into anger. She stood and faced Quinn. "Obviously, there's a reason I'm not in jail. Maybe a little thing like evidence is standing between you and your desire to see me on the gallows?"

Pierce moved forward and slid a hip on the edge of the table. Lounging like that, he was still above the locked glare of the two women. "I'm not sure they still hang people in L.A. And it'd be hard to convince a lynch mob that you'd managed to stab Mr. Montgomery and get no blood on any part of you."

Dee paled. "Stabbed?" Alex Pierce now had her full attention. "But that means somebody planned on killing him."

The detective shook his head. "Not necessarily. He had a tackle box beside his bed."

Dee nodded. "When I called him, Steve mentioned he was going fishing with a buddy up at Castaic tomorrow. That's why we were meeting today."

It was Pierce's turn to nod. "It was a very well equipped box. Only one thing was missing. There was an empty leather sheath. You know what a fillet knife is?"

"Sure. A good one's so thin and sharp a little kid can slice open a shark."

"Or a man."

Chapter 21

"You look like something the hound dog left on the side of the road." Felicia was framed by the doorway of Dee's kitchen.

"It's that glow you get when you've found a dead body and been yelled at by members of the LAPD for an hour."

"I see by your empty living room that you haven't gotten around to refurnishing yet."

Dee dragged clean clothes from the washer and threw them into the dryer. "I won't need to bother if I'm housed at taxpayer's expense for the next ninety years of my life."

Felicia rescued a fallen sock and tossed it in with the rest. "You didn't check to make sure all the spots were removed or that the clothes are all turned right side out. You must really be upset."

Dee slammed the dryer door. "I hate being made to feel incompetent."

"You hate being made to feel weak," Felicia corrected. "Just like I hate being made to feel like a fool."

"A fool? How does any of this make you feel foolish?"

"Your stuff doesn't. Jenny's does."

Dee shut the door to the laundry room. "That's the last load and this sounds like a discussion that needs fresh air and sunshine. Come with me."

The two women grabbed glasses of lemonade from the refrigerator and settled themselves on deck chairs in the shade of an orange tree in Dee's back yard. Sunlight floated through the stiff green leaves casting indefinite shadows across their bodies.

Dee focused on Felicia's face and noted more cream than coffee today in her skin tone. "So what's going on with you and Jenny?"

"I'm a lesbian. My whole life I've been a lesbian."

Since this was not a news flash, Dee just waited.

Felicia ripped her napkin into confetti. "How would you feel if the woman you loved turned out to be a man? My God," she said, head in hands, "does this mean I'm heterosexual?"

Dee fought down a laugh as she sorted through Felicia's words. "Somehow, I don't think so. Does Jenny know about how you feel?"

"Girlfriend, that woman can't take a hint. You'd have to hit Jenny with a twenty pound sack of flour and then dance naked on a table just to get her attention. At least that's what that hussy Sheila seems to have done. Mind you, that is not something I could ever see myself doing. Now I don't know whether to be glad or sad."

Dee reached over and stroked the back of Felicia's neck. "This does kind of make you wonder about the difference between loving the person and loving the package they come in."

Dee thought for several minutes before continuing. "It's hard to imagine Jenny as a guy. She's always so feminine she makes me feel like I'm a super butch. But you've got to know that won't cut a lot of ice with some people."

"That may be true," Felicia said. "People do have this thing about a hound dog being a hound dog even when it's clearly not a hunter. They don't take too kindly to change. And just because she went and got herself physically and legally made a woman doesn't make her so to some people. Won't even matter to them if she gets her birth certificate changed."

"You're right," Dee said. "And there are sisters who won't feel she belongs in our community no matter what."

Felicia sighed. "Oh lordy, I didn't think about all those other lesbians out there. We can be an opinionated lot. Poor Jenny."

"And poor you if you hook up with her. Gee, let's count the reasons the world at large could hate you: you're female, lesbian, black, and in love with a transgendered woman. One more and you win a toaster." Dee smiled grimly. "Sure you want to take all that on?"

"I can see why Jenny left home with no forwarding address. Lord, it makes me tired to think about and I didn't go through any of it." Felicia hugged her arms around herself then sat up. She drew in a deep breath of the warm spring air. "I guess I'll face that when and if Jenny comes to her senses and notices wonderful little ole me." She slapped Dee's knee. "Be that as it may, I can't believe I'm all hang dog and you're the one with the real problems."

"What is it about the South and dogs? All of your expressions use canines. Why not cats or birds or squirrels?"

Felicia gave a half smile. "And who just changed the subject? But since you did, I found out a few things about our news director on that fateful Friday."

Felicia had finally cornered Curtis' secretary, Gloria. He had a meeting scheduled with an advertiser that afternoon, but had Gloria cancel it when he was suddenly called into a meeting with the network president.

"Gloria said he stormed back into the office after the meeting and then went off to look for Rachel. She didn't see him the rest of the day. I don't know for sure, but that might have been when Curtis got the news that Sheila was leaving."

"Then why would he be angry? He didn't like her and it would clear the way for Rachel to step up."

Felicia shook her head. "Maybe the president didn't want Rachel stepping up. That might have put some starch in Curtis' longjohns."

"That would sure explain his rather disgruntled attitude at the wake." Dee heard a ding and jumped out of her chair. "I've got a few things to tell you, too, but that's the dryer. Come with me and I'll fill you in on all the gory details."

Dee chronicled yesterday's events as the women folded the clothes. She added, "I only got one snippet from Quinn and I'm sure she didn't mean to let it out. It seems the motorcycle did belong to Steve, but it was a Harley. Of course that doesn't mean that Mr. Shelbourne couldn't have borrowed it for a few hours."

"Kind of hard to mistake a Hog for a Yamaha, isn't it? Or are you so far down in the marsh that a passing twig seems like a life preserver?"

"Other than Jenny, the only other person we know who was around Sheila's condo that night was Steve. So now that both my prime suspects have been taken out of consideration, I seem to be out of possible bad guys."

A loud ring interrupted Dee's train of thought. Since that train was stalled at the station, she didn't mind answering the telephone. Until she heard Tully's news.

"She what? When? We'll be right there."

"What was all that about?" Felicia demanded.

"It's Jenny. Tully said the police have just arrested her for Sheila's murder."

Chapter 22

The cold concrete of the police station looked just as unwelcoming to Dee as on any of her previous visits. But shock seemed to coat the building with an additional aura of oppression.

Dee and Felicia ran up the wide steps to the double wooden doors of the old Public Works building. Inside, Tully sat hunched on a bench by the wall. One look at her buddy convinced Dee that she was not alone in her forebodings.

Tully looked up. "They're processing Jenny. Nobody can see her right now."

"What do they have on her? How did they even learn of her connection to Sheila?" More questions spun through Dee's cluttered mind, but Tully didn't look capable of answering more than two at a time.

"I'm not sure. We'll know more when Marsha comes out."

"Marsha Brown? Good grief. That woman is going to think we have a homicidal band of friends." Dee sank onto the bench beside Tully. "Did you call her?"

Tully nodded. "I didn't know what else to do. So I called her and then I called you two."

The three women sank into silence. Tully stared at her clasped hands. Felicia leaned against the faded white stucco wall. Dee paraded all the possible suspects through her mind, trying to see the angle that made the facts point to someone besides her—or Jenny.

Felicia had obviously been mulling over the facts as well. She broke the silence. "Dee, you didn't say anything to those detectives did you? The last time they brought you in, you said you shared a lot of the information we'd put together. Was one of those pieces Jenny?"

Tully swung to regard Dee. "You were kind of mad at Jenny for not talking to you. But you wouldn't, you didn't…" Her voice trailed off, but her gaze didn't leave Dee's face.

Dee's jaw worked soundlessly for a moment. "Great," she finally exploded, "just great. Not only do the cops think I bumped off Sheila, but my friends think I'd throw our pal to these wolves in exchange for a 'Get Out of Jail Free' card."

"The police don't think you killed Sheila anymore." Marsha Brown's crisp voice broke into the discussion. "They are quite convinced that Jenny is the murderer."

She placed her briefcase at her feet and crossed her arms before continuing. "It seems that fingerprints belonging to a Kenneth James Felton, Jr. were on the door handle of Sheila's condo as well as a heavy brass statuette, which just happens to be the murder weapon. It took the police a while to find a match for the prints and then to track down the legal papers changing Kenneth James to Jenny, but they did."

"So what?" Tully demanded, rising to her full height. She bested Marsha by a full three inches, but Marsha didn't seem intimidated at all. Tully continued, "That dog won't hunt. Jenny could have left those fingerprints anytime. And having a sex change operation isn't a crime."

Marsha regarded Tully with a cool gaze. "The police also say they have witnesses who saw Jenny leaving Sheila's condo that evening. In addition," she held up one finger to forestall Tully's further objections, "it seems you all were right about one thing. Sheila has written a book. And Jenny's in it."

The four women sat around a Formica booth of the coffee shop across from the police station. Marsha, Felicia, and Tully

Jane DiLucchio

sipped coffee while Dee watched the ice melt in her iced tea.

Dee spoke first. "So you're saying that this literary agent contacted the police regarding Sheila's manuscript? And it for sure includes Jenny?"

"That's what they're saying. I won't get a look at it until we file for discovery." The lawyer frowned as she sipped her coffee. She reached across the table and tore open another sugar packet. "They admitted that the agent only has an outline and a few sample chapters. So it probably doesn't name a lot of people. The agent claims to have gently suggested to Sheila that the manuscript needed work. He figured that was why he hadn't heard back from her."

Felicia nodded. "That must have fried her bacon. She wasn't one to take criticism well. So Sheila must have been floating her book around, trying to find an agent who could get her an advance from a publisher."

Dee considered this news. It meant that her scenario regarding Sheila inviting her over to celebrate the imminent publication of her book was wrong. But someone must not know that or why would he or she break into Dee's home?

"There's got to be something damaging about someone else in that book. Look what somebody did to my house just to make sure Sheila's memoirs never saw the light of day." Dee slapped the table. "That's it. That proves Jenny isn't the murderer." She felt a grin spread across her face. The first glimmer of hope was surfacing. "Jenny wouldn't have torn apart my office looking for the manuscript because she knew it didn't exist."

As the women exited the coffee shop, Dee spotted a very familiar face wandering down the block from the parking lot. "Hey!" she called and waved to Evie Taylor.

"What's going on?" Evie asked as she joined the group. After gathering hugs from Tully and Felicia, she stood, arms crossed, facing Dee. "You're not back in trouble, are you?"

Dee shook her head, but before she could elaborate, Marsha broke in.

"I'll tell you all about it later," Marsha said, as she came up beside Evie and slipped an arm around her shoulders.

Dee stood rooted, watching as Evie smiled up into Marsha's face. Marsha called something to the group as she led Evie away, but it didn't register with Dee.

Only one thought formed in Dee's mind. It involved murder.

Chapter 23

"You just don't get it, do you?" Dee stretched her body to its fullest extent and poked her finger into the impassive face of Gina Quinn. "There's no way Jenny would have broken into my house looking for something she knew didn't exist. That would be too stupid to believe."

Dee had burst into the police station just as Quinn was trying to leave. The vision of Evie and Marsha together had created a fire in Dee that exploded when she spied the detective. Quinn had no choice but to listen.

The detective shoved her hands in the pockets of her blue slacks. "Maybe she was trying to throw you off her trail. After all, didn't you just find out she had been to Shelbourne's condo?"

The police station waiting area was almost deserted, but Dee and the policewoman stood in a corner away from the teenaged mother nursing her infant and a white haired man with shell-shocked eyes. A gaunt-faced young man with stringy orange hair bounced off Dee as he made his way unsteadily towards the Information Desk. Uniformed police and business-suited men and women raced through, but none of them paused until one officer came out and called a name. When the man on the bench didn't respond, the officer came to him, gently wrapped an arm around his shoulder, and led him into the back of the station. The humanity of the gesture contrasted sharply in Dee's mind with her current exchange.

"What about the bike? Jenny can't ride a motorcycle worth

beans. I know. I tried to teach her and she ended up with a face full of flowers after landing in a planter strip. No way could she be the driver."

"Did it ever occur to you that these incidents aren't related to the murder? That's the way the Captain and the D.A. are figuring it." Quinn ran her hand across her eyes. "As far as they're concerned, your attacks are just that—random attacks. They're being reassigned to the Assault and Robbery divisions."

Dee slammed her hand against the wall. Both mother and child stopped their feeding to stare, but Dee ignored them. "What about Steve Montgomery's murder? Is the D.A. ignoring that, too?"

Quinn's voice had more gravel in it than ever before. "Look, the police investigate. The district attorney decides the charges and prosecutes. Sometimes they ask our opinion. Sometimes they even listen."

"And sometimes they don't?" Dee asked.

Quinn looked away. "I've got to go or I'll be late picking up David again." She picked up her shoulder bag then swung back to Dee. "Tell your friends not to do any damn fool thing that will just make it worse for Jenny. Charges may have been filed, but we keep investigating until there's a conviction."

Dee felt her anger cooling. "In that case, we'll keep in touch." Then, she couldn't resist. "I'm sure Tully won't mind being the point person."

Gina Quinn glanced heavenward and gave a slight snort. "I've got to go."

That's all the opening Tully will need, Dee thought, as she watched the handsome detective stride out the front door of the station. Whoever this David guy is, he'd better watch out.

Dee drummed her fingers on the steering wheel of her trusty purple Hyundai. As relieved as she was to know Quinn and Pierce weren't satisfied, she wasn't about to leave it in their hands.

She ran her mind over Sheila's murder. The only motive that stood out was the autobiography. But what could that have to do with Steve? Sheila and Steve had had no contact since San Diego. Dee sat up so straight her mother would have been proud. What was the name of that grip or whatever who knew Sheila back then?

Names were not Dee's strong suit. Whereas other teachers memorized all thirty of their students' names in one or two days, it always took her two weeks. Now, that particular weakness came back to haunt her.

Frustrated, she revved her engine and threw her car into first gear. She may not remember the name, but she knew where to find the woman.

"Don't know what more I can tell you." A well-muscled arm swung a light pod onto a metal stand. Aurora Blacksmith tested the sturdiness of her creation before turning to Dee again. "Sheila and I didn't last much longer after Montgomery threatened mayhem. Sheila landed the job up here and I moved on to the studios. When I decided to go back into TV, I just happened to end up working with her again. Definitely nothing that was planned on either of our parts."

Dee nodded. She had already decided that Aurora could serve as a pin-up model. A couple of inches taller that Dee, Aurora was amply endowed and had flawless blue-black skin, a close-cropped Afro, large, dark eyes, and a glorious smile.

"Did you know any of the other people at the station before coming here to work?"

"The 'Business' is a small one. I knew a lot of the techs and some of the talent."

"How about Rachel O'Neil?"

Aurora flashed a quick smile. "Hadn't the pleasure. But I wouldn't mind." She hefted another light pod onto a second stand. "Did know her husband, though. Worked the same show in San Diego."

"You mean Curtis worked with Sheila down south?"

"Yeah. Wasn't the first time, either." She shook the stand then adjusted the bolts when the pod wobbled. "They knew each other in college."

"How did they get along?"

"Oil and water. That is, when they weren't being flint and stone. Awful competitive, even over the silliest things. Started with some sort of junior reporter award and just bloomed from there."

"Curtis was a reporter?"

"Something like that. You gotta remember, this was six years ago. And Curtis wasn't exactly our primary topic of conversation, if you know what I mean." She flashed another grin at Dee.

"Did they see each other socially?"

"Once in a while. But not real regular. Not even when he was dating Natalie."

Dee had to dust off the file cabinet of her mind. Natalie. Sheila's suicidal sister. Alliteration aside, Dee had let this facet of the saga lapse. Taking a deep breath she reminded herself that it was a good thing she made her living teaching rather than detecting. Too many details to hold in the forefront of a fragile mind.

"Curtis dated Sheila's sister? Were they still dating when she died?"

"Yeah. You know she killed herself? I hear he took it hard at first." She paused in thought, shook her head, then said, "Recovered fast."

"Was there any suggestion at the time that it wasn't suicide?"

"You mean like Curtis killed her?" Aurora scoffed. "No way. Not his style."

"What is his style?"

Aurora leaned against a railing of one of the multitudinous steel ramps leading to and from each sound stage. She popped a breath mint and chewed on it for a moment before answering. "Impulsive, charming. Quite the ladies' man. Talks fast and smoothes the waters. Think that's how he got Rachel to marry him only seven weeks after meeting."

Dee chewed on this as Aurora chewed on another mint. She considered returning to Natalie's death, but Aurora didn't seem to harbor any suspicions about it. The chance to get a somewhat unbiased view of Curtis was too tantalizing.

"How is Curtis as a co-worker?"

"There's good and bad in everyone."

Aurora paused so long Dee feared she was going to leave it with that enigmatic comment. Finally, she continued. "One year he threw a catered party for the whole crew when we gained five points in the ratings. When we slipped two points, he fired four of the hands. Said the look of the show made us lose viewers. Got rid of one of the roving reporters for not covering stories the right way."

Dee said, "That makes sense. I mean, doesn't a director have the responsibility for all those aspects of the show?"

Aurora crunched the last of the mint. "Would have made sense if it hadn't been Curtis who told the reporter which slant to take on the story. I was there and heard him give the instructions."

Dee turned this bit of Curtis' character over in her mind. "Did Curtis and Steve Montgomery ever meet?"

"Sure. Stevie boy always used to hang around the set when he wasn't teaching."

Somehow Dee didn't think the nickname was an endearment. "Did they get along?"

The lighting tech snorted. "Men. Always buddy-buddy. Went fishing together, even rode their cycles into the hills on weekends. Must say, Curtis was all sympathy to Steve when the great coming-out occurred. At least on the surface."

"You got the feeling he enjoyed the whole mess?"

Aurora nodded. "Little gleam in his eye. Nothing said, but

you just knew."

A flatbed truck pulled up with a load of cables. Two husky men jumped down and started flinging the thick black ropes from the truck to the ground by one of Aurora's light stands. Aurora watched, but didn't offer to help.

Dee asked, "Is this part of the shoot you're doing?"

"Yeah. They're stringing the electrical."

"Do you have to go help them?"

Aurora laughed. "Be fired in a minute. Crossing crafts. Big no-no."

Returning to her list of suspects, Dee said, "You mentioned you didn't know Rachel before getting this job. Have you gotten to know her here?"

"Not much. Real driven. Always working on stories, tips, special reports. More like a real news reporter than a lot of the fashion plate, talking heads around here."

"I got the idea she and Sheila were close."

"If so, it'd be more on Rachel's part than Sheila's, if you know what I mean." Aurora seemed to ponder for a moment. "Sheila had a way with women, no denying, and she wasn't heartless. Just had no clue how to be part of a couple. Gave everything of herself—time, energy, money, attention—while she was with you. But when she wasn't, it's like you didn't exist. Makes it hard."

Dee nodded. "When we broke off, Sheila said something about me being a one-woman woman and that was a quality she wished she possessed."

Aurora agreed. "Can't see Rachel liking that."

"But you don't know her well enough to know for sure?"

"Nope. And it doesn't look like I'll get to, either."

"Why not?"

Aurora looked surprised. "Haven't you heard? She got the New York job."

Chapter 24

"The lowdown is that she's going to be a correspondent for the national news. Wait." Felicia held up an embroidered fringed pillow. "What about picking up this blue with the first couch we saw?"

This being the fourth thrift store in three hours, Dee could no longer remember the name of the first store, let alone the color of the sofa. She sank into an overstuffed leather side chair and sighed. "I seem to be missing the shopping gene. Maybe it's run off with my sense of color."

"Along with your sense of style, rhythm, and humor."

"Why don't we rest a minute and you can fill me in on Rachel all at once rather than dribs and drabs between fabric discussions."

"You just have no stamina, girl. Much good all that running and huffing and puffing does you when it comes to real life needs." But Felicia sat, bringing the pillow along. "Here's the whole enchilada in a nutshell."

Dee was so grateful to be sitting and not shopping that she didn't even try to untangle that one.

The day had started with Tully reporting in on Jenny. Bail had been set and Tully met it, but keeping the news hounds away from Jenny was another matter. The police were not revealing any details about the arrest, but it seemed just a matter of time before someone got on the scent of Jenny's past.

Jenny's release seemed to galvanize Felicia. She hit the

rumor circuit at the station and picked up some choice bits.

Rachel had announced her imminent departure after Felicia had left for the day. But Felicia found out that Rachel's leaving seems to have been a shock to everyone, not excluding her hubby, Curtis.

"I wish I had been there to check out their faces. Lord love a duck, but they all must have been more surprised than a chicken who gave birth to a cow."

The grapevine had it that Rachel had the job because of Sheila's demise, but Felicia wasn't too sure. "After all, Sheila was after a desk jockey spot, and Rachel's going to do corre-spondence. Not quite the same league."

"So Rachel seems to be the one to check out. Why the move? Why now? Is it connected to Sheila?" Dee picked up the pillow Felicia had between them without really seeing it. "She did say something about not getting Sheila's anchor spot because of her possible New York jump. So that must have been in the works before Sheila's death."

"Unless she was trying to throw you off the scent."

"The only scent I had at that time was her perfume. A rather spicy fragrance, as I recall. Anyway, sounds like Ms. O'Neil would be worth talking to."

"I could arrange for her to come to my house for a cut. She's not one of my regular clients, but you'd be surprised how many people are willing to accept a free session. I'll say it's a going away present."

Dee smiled. "Hard to walk out in the middle of a haircut."

"Too true, sister. Now that that's settled, let's head on over to Out of the Closet. If someone with your good taste donated stuff to them, there should be gobs of goodies to choose from."

Exhausted from a mere five hours of looking at every thrift store and bargain shop in West Hollywood, Dee threw herself on her bed and stared at the ceiling. She and Felicia had selected a couch, three upholstered chairs, a dining room set, a desk, side tables, and a half dozen accent pieces before Felicia had declared herself satisfied for the day. Dee groaned at the thought that Felicia wasn't done. She herself was content to live in a barren hovel if the alternative was another all-day shopping trip.

She reached beside her for the one find of the day that was hers—a Peruvian rain stick. Dee gently tilted the long stick back and forth and listened as, inside the hollow center, tiny seeds clattered over thorns producing a sound very reminiscent of water flowing over river rocks or falling on the leaves of a tree.

Dee was still idly waving the rain stick a half hour later when the telephone rang. With a lazy stretch she pulled the phone to her ear, then sat bolt upright.

"Steve Montgomery had two motorcycles licensed to him?"

"Right good buddy." Tully's grin came shooting across the wires. "That Harley was his newest bike. Guess that's why he was storing it in the Palisades. Less crime there than North Hollywood."

Dee ignored the irony. "But you're sure the other one was a Yamaha?"

"Sure thing. Three years old. Black."

Dee chewed her lip as she considered this new variable. "It would make him a great suspect."

"Yep. Too bad he's dead."

Knowing that Tully had not meant it as a personal tribute, Dee tried to fit the bike to each person on her list of suspects. Could one of them have borrowed or even stolen Steve's motorcycle? But if Steve stored the Harley with his ex-father-in-law, then that meant the Yamaha was with him.

Tully had said the bike was found in the underground garage of Steve's apartment building. Who could have gotten it there and used it without Steve knowing? Or did he know? Dee thought of *Murder on the Orient Express*. Maybe they all did it together.

Dee flashed to her conversation with Detective Quinn. "The police seem to think there could be two different crimes. Let's say Steve tried to run me down and then tore apart my house trying to get the book because he thought Sheila had told me some secret and had included it in her book. And somebody else killed Sheila for an entirely different reason."

Tully grunted. "And then Steve just happened to commit hari kari with his fishing knife—somehow managing to throw it away before dying. Or do you think a different somebody just happened to kill Steve? I have always heard L.A. was a dangerous place to live, but your scenario makes me want to lock all my doors and never leave the house."

Dee flopped back on her bed. "Miss Marple would have this figured out by now."

"She had the luxury of knowing everyone in town and their family history back several generations. We're a bit short on that kind of info."

"Maybe it's time to get some."

Tully paused before saying, "What's popping into the fertile brain of yours?"

"Do you think Jenny would be up to doing some digging?"

"If it would point out the real killer, she'd dig to China and back."

"I need to know how Sheila's sister died. Medical reports, not just newspaper accounts."

"Even though she's been relieved of her duties as public relations director for the hospital, she still has her contacts in the field, so that should be pretty easy."

Dee continued. "I also want to know when, where, and how Sheila met Steve, Curtis, and Rachel. And maybe she can find out which shrink Sheila and her sister Natalie saw after the molestation. If it was here in L.A., there must be rumors in the community."

"Maybe Evie could help us out there."

Dee felt a twist deep in her stomach. She waited for it to

ease before answering.

Tully jumped into the breech. "That scene with the lawyer can't mean anything. Marsha's just not Evie's type."

"Right. Marsha's intelligent, sophisticated, and wealthy. Nah, not Evie's type at all."

"That's right, good buddy. She prefers the earthy, poor, and medium IQ ones like you."

Dee dragged the phone cord over to her bedroom window and breathed deep of the orange blossom perfume filling the air. "You know just how to cheer a girl up. That must be why you've made such inroads with the lovely detective Gina."

"What kind of inroads might these be?"

"Lord, if you don't know, why should I let you in on her little secrets? But if I were you, I'd watch out for David."

"David?" Tully's voice was wary.

"Yep. And speaking of inroads, why don't we ask Felicia to help Jenny on our research project?"

"Sure, but why?"

"You never can tell where a little collaborative learning assignment may lead."

Chapter 25

Streams of sunlight were tinting the heavy morning clouds with pink when Dee started along the jogging path on Chandler Boulevard. She could remember when this was an active railroad line. The Southern Pacific trains had hauled cargo and supplies up and down this median strip since long before Dee moved to Burbank. One time, Dee followed the time-honored tradition of placing a penny on the tracks. When the passing train had flattened it into a thin piece of metal, she was as thrilled as any child.

But the Southern Pacific tracks were gone, and the city had converted the strip into a walking and jogging path with separate lanes for bicyclists. The young trees were just beginning to fill out enough to provide shade from the almost summer sun, but Dee was not concerned with the heat since she had chosen early morning for her first run since the attack.

The median strip had never been her regular route since it was a mile and a half from her home, so she felt safe being alone somewhere no one would suspect her to be. That, combined with no corner-crossing nightmares, made her relax into her run sooner than she had anticipated.

Her muscles responded with joy to the old routine even while her head got busy with sorting. Rachel had jumped at Felicia's offer of a free cut. Dee needed to be prepared when she had a chat with the lovely redhead this afternoon.

How well did Rachel know Steve? Were they involved in a

romance as well? It didn't seem likely since Rachel appeared more interested in her affair with Sheila than in her marriage.

A blue motorcycle roaring down Chandler turned Dee's thoughts to the attack. Who could have known where she lived? Would her address be in the day planner that the murderer had stolen from Sheila's condo? Even so, how did they know her jogging route? Why attack her on the street when they could just wait until she had left the house and searched for the manuscript then? Did someone have a vendetta against her, too?

That manuscript! Dee's thoughts ran faster than her feet. The person obviously didn't know exactly what was in the manuscript. They couldn't have known it was just fifty pages and an outline as that lawyer person (Dee's brain refused to acknowledge Marsha's name) had reported to Jenny. Or was there really an entire book, and Sheila had only sent part to the agent?

Who wanted Sheila dead? It made Curtis' life easier in many ways and freed up the opportunity for his wife to take the lead anchor position. On the other hand, that might have been a good motive for Rachel, except she now was heading to New York. Would she lose something besides her marriage, which she seemed to be running away from, if Sheila's book were published? Of course, Dee reminded herself, that was presuming a book existed.

Then there were Sheila's parents. Henry certainly had a temper and seemed to blow easily, but why kill his own daughter?

And none of this explained why Steve was killed.

A sudden rustling in the bushes made Dee leap to one side. She grabbed her can of pepper spray and aimed it towards the noise.

The leaves of the bush parted. A brown arm extended from the bush. A furry brown arm.

Dee lowered her defenses as a brown and white tabby pulled itself free of the undergrowth and eyed Dee cautiously.

"Come here girl." Dee knelt on one knee and extended her hand.

The sound the cat emitted reminded Dee of the cabinet in her schoolroom that hadn't been oiled since it was built in 1940. The cat cautiously examined Dee's face. Only then did it come forward and allowed itself to be petted. Dee grinned. The cat rolled its eyes in ecstasy when Dee found that special spot near its ears.

Dee remembered Sheila comparing them both to cats. She had said Dee was like a skittish half-wild kitten, wanting to have a home, but scared to be trapped in one place.

Sheila had said, "Some of us are the exotic type. The kind of cat who would do well in a loving home. But people take the cat in for all the wrong reasons—how cute or how impressive. When they find out about the special needs of the breed, it's back out on the street."

In retrospect, the poignancy gripped Dee. Just whose home did Sheila really want to be part of?

A second rustling in the bushes caused Dee to start. The cat leapt towards the sound.

"Fickle, aren't you?" But Dee was still somber as she started back on her run only to see Jack O'Reilly and his flashing safety vest running towards her.

Today a bright yellow headband encircled his forehead under his grizzly reddish-gray hair. Instead of his usual nod in passing, Jack slowed and walked over to Dee.

"Good to see you out again," Jack said, with a bit of a lilt. "I see you decided this might be a better place to run, too. I tell you, even with my dogs beside me, I couldn't shake that eerie feeling when I ran down Clark. So I told myself, why don't you take yourself up to that little green park they've made on Chandler and do your run there? And so I did, and so I am, and so are you, too, I see."

Jack's brogue made Dee feel like she had wandered into the middle of a St. Paddy's Day parade. "Thank you. I don't know what would have happened if you hadn't been around."

"Stuff and nonsense," Jack broke in. "I did nothing that any other person wouldn't. I just hope they've caught that no good ruffian. Have they now?"

"Not yet. I couldn't give them a very good description."

"Aw, now, as to that, I couldn't either. He just took off like a shot and then turned down Reese. He was gunning his motor and making zigzags all over, so he was really in trouble when he hit that speed bump. Ah," Jack shook his head, "it's too bad he didn't fall. Then I'd have nabbed him for sure."

"You chased him?"

"Aye, for a bit. But I was worried about you and he was fast down the road. I decided it was best to take care of you first and let the constables catch him later. I'm sorry to hear they haven't yet." His mouth was turned down as if the failure of the police to apprehend the suspect somehow reflected on him. "Well, I must be off."

"Wait, Jack. You said the guy had trouble making the turn on to Reese?"

"Well, now. I think he might have been going a wee too fast."

"So he was off balance when he hit the speed bump?"

"Aye. And he almost flew off the bike when he did. That's when I thought I'd have a chance at him. But he was able to pull himself back on. Too bad. I know I could have taken him."

"You really think so?"

"Oh, sure. He was a real lightweight. You should have seen his body fly off the motorbike when he hit the bump. Like a cowboy on a bucking bronco." Jack bent from side to side at the waist. "I'll be off now. Don't you dilly dally. Too hard to get back into things if you stay away too long. Besides, it looks as though we're in for a bit of spring rain later." So saying he leaped off and bounced his way down the path.

Dee had never noticed his accent before. But that wasn't surprising since they had done no more than exchange names once when they'd both stopped for water, and ever after, nodded or just said hello in passing.

So the motorcycle driver was a lightweight. And possibly

inexperienced on a bike. The lightweight part should leave Jenny in the clear just as the novice aspect condemned her.

Dee decided to head home. She'd have to quietly sort through everything before talking with Rachel later that morning. This may be her only chance.

Chapter 26

"The worst part was, I almost ran into the killer." Dee dramatically smacked her hands together and waited for the reply.

"Really?" Rachel O'Neil raised one eyebrow, but kept her head carefully still under Felicia's scissors. "So you saw that Feldman woman come out? Is that how the police were able to catch her?"

Dee winced both at the mangling of Jenny's name and the idea that she herself was somehow responsible for Jenny's apprehension. "Not exactly. But I'm sure I must have seen the murderer or at least his car. But since that bump on my head, I have trouble remembering some things."

Dee and Felicia had discussed their line of questioning for half an hour before Rachel had shown up. Dee's presence was excused on the grounds that she had just received a trim from Felicia. She hung around at Felicia's enthusiastic, and Rachel's half-hearted, invitation.

So far Rachel showed no guilty knowledge. She seemed sympathetic concerning Dee's concussion and the destruction in her home, as well as concerned over her finding Steve Montgomery's body. But there had been no remorseful slip of the tongue. The only item Rachel had dropped was that she had been interviewing the mayor of Long Beach at the time of Steve's death. She had stayed overnight to attend a town hall meeting the next day. Dee figured that would be easy enough for Felicia to check.

Dee pondered how to find out about Curtis' movements when Felicia turned the subject around.

"Have you lived in New York before?"

"No. I'm a Midwest girl. Iowa born and bred. My family is still in Dancy. That's about seventy miles southeast of everywhere."

"A farm girl!" Felicia sounded delighted. "How did you ever make your way from those green fields to the big city?"

"I got a scholarship to USC. Journalism. I was offered one from Georgetown, but SC had a better financial package, so I took it. I've often wondered if I missed something not going to school in Washington."

"Being a roving reporter you might just get to spend a lot of time in D.C. after all," Dee suggested.

Rachel gave a wan smile. "Roving reporters don't get to spend a lot of time in any one place."

"Is that why your husband won't be joining you?" Dee tried to make her voice as innocent sounding as possible.

Rachel shrugged. "Curtis' career is here."

"But he's moved around before, hasn't he? Didn't he used to work in San Diego?"

"Sure. But L.A. was a move to a larger market. There's no chance for an equal position for him in New York. He'd kill his career to follow me there." She pulled on her bangs and said to Felicia, "How about just a smidgen more off here? And a little lighter around the neck?"

As the two women discussed the pros and cons of fluffing, waving and other items of non-interest to a person with inch-long hair, Dee stared out the window and sorted through the facts. Rachel hadn't exactly said that she and Curtis were calling it quits, but a bi-coastal marriage with at least one bisexual partner did not sound like a recipe for domestic bliss.

Felicia's voice pulled Dee back to the room.

"Did you and Sheila plan to room together while you both got settled back East?"

Felicia's innocent tone combined with the innocuous phrasing gained Dee's admiration and seemed to disarm Rachel as well.

"Oh no. Sheila found out about her job days before I learned that I'd be going to New York, too."

"But you knew Sheila was up for the job?"

"Sure. We talked about it. She knew I wanted to move as well. But those network jobs rarely crack. It just so happened that two openings popped at the same time. Pure luck I guess."

"Maybe fate," Dee suggested.

Rachel raised an eyebrow.

"You two were thrown together here in L.A. without ever knowing each other before. Then you both get coveted East Coast jobs at the same time. Maybe the gods had something in mind."

"If so, their timing is lousy."

Rachel quickly swung the dentist chair back around, but not before Dee saw her jaw muscles flex and tighten.

Dee decided to switch topics fast. "Are you driving to New York with all your things?"

Felicia's look suggested that Dee had just landed with a shipload of Martians.

"No," Rachel replied. "A car won't be of much use there. I'm thinking of getting a bike."

Dee smiled. "You're going to be one of those Manhattan peddlers like the guys who deliver messages across town?"

Rachel shook her head. "Not for me. I'm thinking a scooter or maybe even a Harley. That would really show those guys how to really cut through traffic."

"Why would Rachel bash Dee and search her house? What's she got to lose being in Sheila's book?" Jenny thumped her leg with a rolled up "Good Housekeeping" and frowned. The friends had descended on Felicia's house as soon as Rachel left. The debate raged from the moment they all sat down.

Jenny used the magazine to brush some lint from her blue cotton slacks and then continued. "Of course, that's presuming we buy Tully's rather lurid account of lust and betrayal between Sheila and Rachel."

"All I said, good buddy, was that Rachel didn't hear about her job until after Sheila's death." Tully creaked back in an old rocking chair and threw her arms wide. "Maybe she killed Sheila to get her New York deal."

Felicia shook her head. "First of all, it was a different position. Sheila was getting an anchor slot. Rachel's going to be a reporter. Secondly, I can't believe that a woman who'd weep at the thought of Sheila's death could possibly be a cold-blooded murderer."

"That argument's all hat and no cattle," Tully jumped in. "It wasn't cold blooded. It was a heat of the moment, passionate type kill. And that redhead is certainly passionate."

Dee twirled around in Felicia's dentist/hairdressing chair. She felt like the circles in her head were representative of the swirling arguments the other three women had been having for the last fifteen minutes.

"You do realize," Dee said at last, "that, number one, Rachel was on television the night Sheila was killed and, number two, she doesn't own a motorcycle and has no clear connection with the one in Steve's garage."

In the small silence that greeted her words, Dee imagined she heard the sound of air escaping from balloons.

"Well, that's not quite right." Felicia broke the silence. She explained that Rachel did fill in for the six o'clock anchor. However, Curtis' secretary reported that before pulling his own disappearing act, Curtis pulled Rachel from the five o'clock and sent her on a high profile on-the-spot reporting job for the earlier news. "So she was working both newscasts, but she did have some unaccounted-for time."

Jenny whacked her leg again and stood. "I realize that means Tully is ready to make a citizen's arrest on Rachel, but I think we need to look at everything together. Felicia and I have been working on our research assignment and I think we've found some interesting items." She brought out her briefcase and unsnapped the locks. Xeroxed copies of newspaper articles, legal papers, and medical files spilled forth.

Felicia leapt forward to catch the pile and Jenny smiled her thanks. The two lifted the papers out together. As they placed the stack on the coffee table, Dee thought their hands lingered in touch a moment longer than necessary.

Jenny cleared her throat. "First of all, Sheila, Steve, and Curtis all met at San Diego State University. That's also where Curtis met Sheila's sister, Natalie. Curtis was the only guy Natalie dated for more than a month or two."

Felicia and Jenny alternated in explaining about the four people and their college careers. Sheila and Curtis majored in Mass Communication, Steve and Natalie in Biology. The older three were highly honored at graduation. This resulted in Sheila and Curtis getting hired at the local television station and Steve going on to study for his doctorate at UC San Diego.

"Meanwhile, Natalie, who was a year behind, was finishing up her B.A. and looking forward to med school at UCLA." Jenny paused. "That's when she supposedly committed suicide."

Felicia nodded. "It appears she overdosed using a combination of Valium and sloe gin, both of which were hers. Seems she had a 'nervous condition' as well as an ulcer and a love of liquor."

Jenny picked up the thread. "There were four things that seemed to interest the police. One, was the fact that she had apparently engaged in a sexual liaison right before death."

Tully snorted. "If it was with Curtis, that would be enough reason to kill yourself right there."

Ignoring Tully's contribution, Jenny continued.

"The second interesting bit was that there was no suicide note."

Dee perked up. "That looks fishy."

Felicia nodded. "The police thought so too. Especially in light of the third item. There were bruises on Natalie's arms and cheek."

Dee held up a hand. "Couldn't that mean that her suicide was faked? Like somebody lifted her into that noose?"

Jenny nodded. "They looked into that possibility. Particularly since sounds of yelling were reported and a man was seen leaving her room an hour before her body was found."

"And just who was this mysterious visitor?" Tully prompted.

"None other than Mr. Henry Shelbourne."

Chapter 27

Despite the darkening clouds stacking up beside the Verdugo Mountains, Dee headed her Hyundai over the hills towards Pacific Palisades. It looked as though Jack's prediction of a rainstorm might be accurate, but Dee decided that driving over wet and oil-slicked roads was nothing compared to the slippery clues she was trying to follow.

Figuring that the Welcome Wagon would not greet her at the Shelbourne house, she had not called ahead. But luck was with her when Mrs. Shelbourne was the one who answered the door and asked her in.

Dark circles ringed Amanda Shelbourne's eyes and deep lines spread outward from their edges. Her tone held life even though her face belied it. "I remember you from the funeral. You were very kind."

Dee was thankful that Mr. Shelbourne had evidently not seen fit to share the contents of her last visit. She offered her condolences again as she sank down into the white couch.

The starkness of the living room was even more glaring to Dee now that the funeral flowers were gone. Only the faint outlines of the green plants showing through the white sheers at the windows relieved the coldness of the room.

Looking at the grieving woman who had settled on the couch beside her, Dee decided honesty might be the best approach.

"I presume you've heard about Steve Montgomery."

"Oh yes. I just spoke with his parents yesterday. The funeral is being held in San Diego tomorrow. I suppose I should go, but I just don't think I can."

"I'm sure his family will understand," Dee responded, not at all sure of any such thing. So much for total honesty. She gave it another try. "I was the one who found Steve."

"How terrible for you, dear." Mrs. Shelbourne looked distressed. "Is that why you're here? To find out about the funeral arrangements?"

"Actually, I wanted to ask you about Steve. He mentioned how close he felt to you and your husband, despite the divorce."

Mrs. Shelbourne smiled. "Steve was such a good boy. I never did understand their problems, but even after they separated, we stayed close. Steve would call and take us to dinner when he was in town and then when he moved to L.A., well, we were so thrilled."

It seemed strange to Dee that Sheila's mother would not understand the reason for the divorce. She wondered if staying close to Steve was a way for the Shelbournes to try to deny their daughter's lesbianism.

"Had you seen him recently?"

"Why yes. He came by last week. He was dropping off his new motorcycle and he stayed for lunch. He and Henry talked on and on about riding and fishing and all those things men like to do. I'm afraid I wasn't following too closely." She sighed and plucked at a loose thread on the side of the couch. "It didn't matter what they were talking about. It was just comforting having them both here."

"I'm sure." Platitudes seemed to be crowding to the forefront of her mind. Dee dug past them to find the line of interrogation she had planned on the drive over. "Did you know of any of Steve's other friends in the area? I'd like to make sure they all know about what happened."

"He had some friends that he had met at his gym, but I'm afraid I don't remember their names. All these names nowadays seem so alike anyway. Biff and Buff and heaven knows what. I also think he was seeing a young lady, but he didn't say much. Oh dear," Mrs. Shelbourne paused and blinked. "That would be you, wouldn't it, dear? Of course, he didn't disclose anything of a personal nature on that front at all."

Dee could tell the older woman was embarrassed at the thought of knowing something about Dee's love life. Dee was even more embarrassed at the thought that the woman thought there was something to know.

Mrs. Shelbourne launched into a fresh round of reminiscences that ranged back to Steve's college days. "You know that Steve dated Natalie before he met Sheila? In fact, that's how they met. Through Natalie. We were so worried about Natalie. She had such troubles with her studies and all at first. But after Steve and Sheila got together, Natalie seemed to settle down and she ended up qualifying for medical school. We were so proud." She smiled and looked off into the distance. Then her face contorted. "Oh, dear. Natalie and Sheila and Steve. All gone before me. That's not the way it's supposed to be."

Dee reached across and placed her fingers atop the veined hand of the older woman. The platitudes deserted Dee and she just sought to send warmth into the soul of the woman who had birthed and lost both Sheila and Natalie.

Mrs. Shelbourne seemed to shake off her melancholy sufficiently to ask Dee if she would like some refreshments. Dee's refusal seemed to be enough of a distraction that their conversation resumed in fits and starts.

After a few more moments of sharing Steve stories, Dee excused herself. As Mrs. Shelbourne was bidding her goodbye, Dee asked, "You mentioned that Steve and your husband were discussing fishing when they last spoke. Did Steve say he was going fishing anytime soon?"

"Yes. He said he wanted to try Castaic and my husband tried to talk him into Golden River instead. Or was it the other way around?"

Before Amanda Shelbourne could debate the matter further, Dee asked if she knew who was going fishing with Steve.

"Why, Henry, of course, and two other friends. It was their group's annual fishing trip."

Dee took the pieces one by one and tried to use her little grey cells to put the pieces together. Henry would know that Steve was home and packing. He would know how to use a filet knife. He drove a black BMW. He had access to a black motorcycle.

But what was the trigger that would cause him to kill Sheila now? Why kill his son-in-law, with whom he seemed to have a cordial relationship? Why would Henry Shelbourne jump on a motorcycle and wield a bat against Dee?

And if he had done it, would he try again? Dee worried about more than the rain-slicked streets during her drive home.

Chapter 28

The Amtrak train whizzed by Fullerton, Santa Ana, and Oceanside as it headed toward San Diego. Dee and Tully reclined in their seats, legs elevated on the foot rests, and drank their complimentary glasses of Merlot. Tully had insisted on Business Class reserved seating for their adventure and Dee was persuaded by logic and the lure of extra comfort. They rehashed their findings and their lines of investigation as the train swayed over the tracks.

Part of Dee's attention was on the official notification she had received lifting her suspension from work. Since she was no longer a murder suspect, the school board felt it wise to bring her back. Dee suspected they were afraid she'd file a lawsuit if they didn't.

Jim Tolkien and the rest of the union negotiations team had kept her informed regarding the lack of progress at the talks. All were eager to have her rejoin them. Dee didn't share their enthusiasm.

Considering her classroom had been in the hands of one or more subs for over a week, her principal and some faculty members still harbored suspicions of her murderous ways, and the school board was rescinding her banishment only reluctantly, Dee had serious doubts as to the wisdom of resuming her post. Mortgage payments seemed to be the only incentive to return.

Dee had used Steve's funeral as an excuse for a personal necessity leave, so had one more day of freedom. If she didn't discover enough information to finish their investigation, she would have to rely on the benevolence and fortitude of Gina Quinn and Alex Pierce.

She hated that idea.

So she and Tully had decided to pursue the San Diego trail in person. They had decided that it would be most appropriate for Dee to attend Steve's funeral, especially if she would be perceived as his latest love interest, while Tully investigated the college angle.

Sun flashed on the crisp blue waves of the Pacific visible through the huge expanse of window beside her. The view did nothing to lighten Dee's mood as she reviewed her list of suspects.

Dee finally shook her head and muttered, "The only motives I can come up with are for the dead people to kill each other."

"That sounds like a promo for a new TV show: *Psychic private eye stalks murderous ghost.* I'll bet the Fox network would pick it up in a heartbeat." Tully angled her body out of her seat, avoiding the low ceiling created by the overhead luggage compartment. "We'd better get our stuff. Next stop is San Diego."

Amid the palm trees and glass buildings that marked the depot, Tully and Dee split up. Dee waved Tully into a taxi bound for San Diego State while she grabbed a cab for the Mission Creek Cemetery.

True to its name, long, low adobe buildings framed the open driveway to the cemetery. Deep green rolling hills pockmarked with white headstones formed the backdrop to the haciendas. At the gate, Dee's driver was directed to the Spanish-styled church at the end of the drive.

Black seemed to be the color of the day. Not among the faces which held a mixture of hues, but in the attire. As Dee passed through the outside throng she noted many young people in attendance. Most looked around as if unsure where they were or why they were there. Dee tagged them as university students experiencing their first brush with death.

Inside, the pews were crowded. A reflection of a life spent as an educator, Dee thought. Not only did your colleagues attend your service, but many current and former students as well. She wasn't sure how comforting that idea was to her.

Dee sauntered slowly up a side aisle. She kept a lookout for an empty seat and, more importantly, familiar faces. She had almost reached the altar when she saw Henry and Amanda Shelbourne. They were seated in the second row directly behind what Dee presumed was Steve's immediate family. Dee watched as Amanda Shelbourne patted the shoulder of the woman in front of her.

A movement in the center aisle caught her attention. Curtis Lee's tall frame caught the multicolored light beaming through the stained glass side windows. He was just settling in beside his wife. He pulled his reading glasses from his left breast pocket of his dove grey suit and started to scan the program.

Dee thought both Curtis and Rachel looked markedly more poised than they had at Sheila's funeral. Rachel, wearing a black short dress which set off her pale skin and red hair, looked composed. Her eyes did not bear any traces of red puffiness. Of course, Dee reasoned, Rachel supposedly only knew Steve through Curtis. Not a close friend. Then why was she down here? Wouldn't it have made more sense for just Curtis to come to mourn his friend?

Dee retreated towards the middle of the church. A group of three slid over the worn and polished wooden bench to make room for her on the aisle. She turned to watch any last minute arrivals and found herself staring into the darkness of Gina Quinn's eyes.

Unreasonable guilt reared in Dee's conscience. Then she made the connection. Detective Quinn reminded her of her catechism teacher, Sister Margaret. Put a wimple on that face and Quinn and Sister Margaret would be twins. She wondered how Tully would like being Captain Von Trapp to Quinn's Maria. Dee grinned at the thought. Gina Quinn frowned in return.

Just as the organ music swelled to a new crescendo, two more people appeared in the church doorway. The sun backlit the entrance of Evie Taylor and Marsha Brown.

"What in blazes do you think you are doing here?"

Detective Quinn's angry hiss caused Dee to splash her glass of 7-Up all over her hand. She shook her wet and sticky fingers and tried to formulate a reply.

The reception hall of the Mission Creek Country Club was even more crowded than the church had been. A bar had been set up in one corner of the room and a long table covered with ivory linen and edibles stretched along the back wall. Both were popular locations.

The floor to ceiling windows, which formed one wall of the room, opened onto the greens of the golf course. The juxtaposition of men and women outside hiking by in their shorts and polo shirts with the somberly clad guests inside the room had held Dee's attention before Gina Quinn's remark had shattered her meditation.

Quinn handed Dee a cocktail napkin. "Well?" Quinn asked, raising her eyebrow.

Dee considered prevaricating, but took the plunge instead. "Same as you, I'd guess. Trying to figure out who killed who and why. And by the way, aren't you a little out of your jurisdiction?"

"At least I have a jurisdiction, which you do not."

Ignoring the gauntlet flung on the floor, Dee changed the subject. "Did you see all our favorite people here? Did you notice that Rachel and Curtis left right after the service?"

"And did you notice your ex come in? With your lawyer?"

Dee gritted her teeth. She had anticipated using the time during Steve's memorial service to analyze and evaluate people's reaction, but her thoughts dwelled instead on vindictive methods of a more personal nature.

Gina Quinn broke Dee's reverie. "What do you think they're doing here?"

"I've been asking myself that for the last hour."

"Maybe it's time to ask them." So saying, Quinn glided across the room to the two women who had just entered the door of the reception hall.

Just as Quinn stopped Evie and Marsha, the door swung open again. Tully almost knocked over the threesome. Tully looked at the group, stared at Quinn, opened her mouth, closed it abruptly, and blushed. She sidled away.

Dee waved her over. "If you're trying to look inconspicuous, you need to lop about six inches off the top of your head and choose a hair color other than white. Wearing something other than bright red might help, too."

"My hair's Moonglow blonde and red is a power color. You saddle up your best horses when riding into enemy territory. Not that you'd know anything about that, sitting here in the lap of luxury, drinking champagne and eating caviar, while I go off and do the dirty work. After all, I risked life and limb, my eyesight, and my eardrum to save my dearest friends from a fate worse than death."

"I thought that was white slavery."

"Whatever cruel fate you were about to succumb to, I have officially rescued you. The least you could do is share your champagne." The last words were accompanied by an attempted snatch of Dee's drink.

"Sorry to disappoint. Nonalcoholic. Thought it would be best if I kept my head clear."

"Considering your eyes haven't left the little manage-a-trois in the corner, I think a good stiff drink might do you some good."

"So distract me with some good news."

Tully grabbed Dee's arm and steered her over to where two armchairs upholstered in green velour nestled in a corner. "I'd rather hide behind some palm fronds, but this will have to do." Tully leaned forward and whispered. "I've broken the case wide open!"

Chapter 29

Dee pushed. "Spill it. Quinn's going to arrest me for being a public nuisance if we don't have something productive soon."

Tully hefted herself onto one hip to pull out a spiral bound notebook from her back pocket. She flipped through the pages and in a poor Joe Friday imitation said, "Just the facts."

Tully settled back and read from her notes. "One Melinda Osgood was one of Natalie Shelbourne's roommates in college. Ms. Osgood is now Director of Student Affairs at San Diego State and remembers her, quote, dearest friend, end quote, quite clearly. According to Ms. Osgood, Natalie was a bit of a party girl. She liked dating better than studying and her grades reflected that. Somehow, despite what should have been a poor grade point average, Natalie was accepted into UC San Diego's medical school."

Dee raised an eyebrow. "Family connections?"

Tully shook her head. "Nope. Melinda Osgood did drop the hint that Natalie was a student worker in Admissions and Records. And that Natalie's boyfriend, whose name she couldn't remember, managed to graduate cum laude when he was known to be an average student."

Now both of Dee's eyebrows shot up. "Did the university suspect someone might be tampering with transcripts?"

"Evidently, yes. Ms. Osgood had many speculations as to the scope and direction of the university's investigation, but no concrete evidence."

"So maybe Natalie was tampering with documents and was about to get caught. That's a scandal her family wouldn't like."

Tully nodded. "Neither would the boyfriend with the tainted transcripts. But it gets better."

A short, stout, balding man disrupted their conference to ask the way to the restroom. Why he thought they would be information central, Dee could not decide, but she used the interruption to sneak a peak at the threesome in the corner. Evie, Marsha, and Detective Quinn were still deeply absorbed in their conversation.

After having dispatched the lost loo seeker, Tully reported that she had obtained the name and address of Natalie's other roommate from the talkative and cooperative Ms. Osgood and was able to interview her as well.

"Liz Buchanan described Natalie as a good kid who just didn't have very good judgment. She seemed to view Natalie as a lost little girl who was competing, and losing, to a driven big sister."

Liz Buchanan had no knowledge of any kind of grade change scheme, nor did she characterize Natalie as a party girl.

"She did admit that Natalie did not do well in classes, but she attributed that to what she described as Natalie's nervousness."

Dee asked, "Did she say why Natalie was so nervous?"

Tully smirked. "Oh, yes. We get a two for one with this one. According to her, Natalie was being abused by her boyfriend and harassed by her parents. In fact, she described Natalie as being on the edge due to the combination of pressure from her grad year, her lover, and, specifically, her father."

Liz Buchanan had gone on to describe the bruises on Natalie's arms when she had returned to the dorm room the night of her suicide. Melinda Osgood was not home that evening and Liz was about to leave for a date.

"She claimed she tried to talk to Natalie about the bruises, but Natalie refused. Since this was not the first time she had bruises after being with her boyfriend, Liz did not push the issue."

"Did she know who the boyfriend was?" Dee asked, wanting her suspicions confirmed.

"She only knew his first name was Curtis."

Dee recalled that the autopsy report said Natalie had engaged in sex before she died. What if that sex had not been consensual?

Tully's voice brought her back to the room. "One other interesting tidbit from Ms. Buchanan. Before she left that evening for a rendezvous with a frat man of high standing, Henry Shelbourne darkened the door of the dorm room. He didn't start yelling until Liz had left the room, but she said the gist of his anger had something to do with the possibility of Natalie being expelled. And when Liz returned from said date, Natalie had done herself in."

"The school must have found out about the grade scam and notified Natalie's parents."

Tully agreed. "The good old boys at the college probably put pressure on the right people to make sure this reason for her suicide never hit the papers. Wouldn't do to let people think grades could be messed with."

"This is great, but how does this tie together with Sheila's murder?"

"Well, now, both roommates also happened to mentioned the interesting little fact that our intrepid reporter Sheila Shelbourne had come visiting two months ago asking very similar questions."

Dee considered Sheila's actions. "Research for her book perhaps? If so, neither Henry nor Curtis would be too pleased with that chapter. But how would they know about it and would exposure of their parts in the tragedy be enough reason for either one of them to kill Sheila?"

"Beats me. I'm just bringing home the doggies. You'll have to brand them."

"You said you solved the case!" Dee's exasperated voice caught the attention of two couples standing a few yards away. She gave them a reassuring smile and turned back to her cohort. Lowering her voice, she said, "How does this solve anything?"

Before Tully could reply, a shadow fell over the two women. Dee sensed the presence without having to look up. She was now convinced that Gina Quinn and Sister Margaret were soul sisters. They could both make her sit straight and look at the floor with just their presence.

Quinn's presence didn't seem to have quite the same effect on Tully. She broke into a wide, welcoming grin. That is, until Gina Quinn spoke.

"I ought to have you two put away for your own safety, if nothing else."

"How sweet of you to worry," Dee said, standing to meet the stare of her tormentor. "We were just about to leave. We have a train to catch, right Tully?"

Tully's face still wore a smile though the wattage had dimmed a bit. "Maybe you'd like to join us? A long cozy ride home might give us all a chance to become better acquainted."

Dee was amazed when Quinn's face softened and almost smiled. "You don't quit, do you?"

"Not when I see what I want."

Electricity, which did not include Dee in its circuit, sparked. Dee slid quietly to the side and left the two tall women in a staring contest.

Swiveling towards the door, Dee saw Marsha and Evie in front of the memorial book. Evie was signing and Dee could imagine the precise and clear handwriting that was so characteristic of Evie. No swirls or dots or curlicues. Just strong and straightforward.

Marsha accepted the pen and signed the book. Dee judged it was a scrawled name rather than one thoughtfully engraved.

The two women left without further goodbyes to anyone in

the room. Dee only half absorbed the comings and goings as the gathering began to break up. Finally Henry and Amanda Shelbourne came forward to sign the book. To her surprise, both the Shelbournes gripped the pen in their left hands and spent several long minutes writing.

Dee closed her eyes and thought. Was Sheila left handed? She didn't think so. Would it be unusual for two lefties to produce a right hander?

"Wake up, old pal. We've got a long ride home to the barn."

Tully's voice caused Dee to jump out of her reverie. "No luck?"

"I told you. It's not luck." Tully pulled Dee out the door and into the hallway. "Ever play a fish on a line? You let them run out a little, then reel them back in, back and forth, till they're too tuckered out to fight."

"So your plan is to exhaust her, then pounce?"

"My plan is to let her realize what she really wants."

"And if that isn't you?"

Tully shook her head. "You are truly one of God's innocent creatures, aren't you? By the way, want to know why your lovely lady and her law school Lothario were here?"

"Marsha killed him and came out of remorse?"

"That wins you a trip to Fantasy Island. In the real world, Marsha was Steve's lawyer. They met when she worked in a law office down here and he was working as a typist while going through graduate school."

"If the world gets any smaller, Walt Disney's going to have to shorten that song."

Ignoring Dee, Tully continued her report. "She also drew up his will. Two little surprises there. One, he specifically left Sheila out of his will."

"That's not really surprising. I'd imagine most ex-husbands don't leave much to their ex-wives."

"That's surprise number two. He and Sheila were never legally divorced."

Chapter 30

Dee drove to school with triple anxiety. Not only was she unsure how to connect the dots of Sheila's murder, but she also knew that in one short hour she would be facing thirty-two fifth graders who had been in the hands of heaven knows how many substitutes. To top it all off, she had no lesson plans.

She unlocked the door of her classroom. Her gaze swept past the expected piles of papers on her desk to absorb the unexpected orderliness of counter tops, bulletin boards, and student desks. She dropped her briefcase on her swivel chair and moved closer to the display headed"Best of the Best." Recent student papers, some dated only two days ago, were mounted. The board was more current than she had ever kept it.

Dee repositioned her briefcase to the side of the desk and sat. Before her lay four stacks, each with a label: Corrected Papers to be Returned, Graded Tests to be Recorded, School Memos, and Notes from Parents. In the center of her desk lay a brief summary of what had been covered in each subject over the past eight days along with a suggestion for today's activities.

Dee studied the desktop. She had no idea who subbed for her, but she wanted to hire that person to organize her life.

She closed her eyes for a moment and remembered her first year of teaching. She had been thrilled to have her own classroom, to arrange and rearrange it, to try new techniques, to spend nights and weekends researching information and gathering manipulatives for units of study. When had teaching changed from a passion to a job? She opened her eyes with a new resolve.

Physical education period was the cap for a glorious day for Dee. The students had been excited to see her again and her lessons had a spark that delighted both the children and the teacher.

The big end-of-the-year softball game between the two fifth grade classes was only a week away so Dee split the class into two squads. The more proficient half of the class ran fielding and batting drills under the direction of the co-captains, Frank and Ana. Dee worked with the weaker group trying to improve their eye-hand coordination. It was an uphill battle.

Dee held the ball and brought it towards the batter as that student slowly swung the bat just to the point of touching the ball. She repeated the exercise several times with each student, bringing the ball in lower, then higher, forcing the batter to watch the ball and not just swing in the same place each time. Then she backed up, bit by bit, and pitched while the student swung gently, just to the point of tapping the ball.

Auburn-haired Heidi, gifted in science but uncoordinated in any physical pursuit, stepped to the plate. Dee had always attributed Heidi's problem to the fact that as the only left-hander in the family, she had been taught to throw and bat right-handed.

Dee had been working all year to correct this with Heidi. Progress crept at its petty pace. Today, however, Heidi was showing signs of brilliance. Every soft pitch was tapped by the bat as Dee backed further and further away. Finally, Dee reached the pitcher's mound.

"All right, Heidi," Dee yelled. "Let her rip!"

Heidi spread her feet, raised her left elbow, gritted her teeth, and kept her eyes on the ball. She swung with every ounce of her seventy pounds.

The ball flew straight and true. Followed closely by the bat.

Dee ducked the ball, but the aluminum bat cracked against her shielding forearm and smacked down an inch from the just healed welt of the motorcycle marauder's strike. Dee went down for the count.

"Oh God!" Heidi screamed. "I killed Ms. DelValle!"

Half the schoolyard formed a ring around Dee's prostrate form. She looked up at Heidi's pallid face. The next face looking down was Jim Tolkien. Then the school nurse. Then a twenty-something-year-old paramedic.

As she answered the paramedic's questions about the date and the presidency, Jim's voice cut through. "This is not going to get you out of today's negotiation session."

Arthur Long, president of the Glendale Unified School Board, more than earned his nickname, Old Long and Dry. Everything about him was long: his face, his nose, his bony fingers, and, especially, his speeches.

Dee hated the sessions when Long was present. Every sentence he uttered was chewed on, considered, reconsidered, and edited twice before it ever emerged from his mouth. Today Dee wanted to leap over the table and pull his tongue out. Only her aching temple kept her stationary and silent.

Long was pontificating on the two options regarding health care coverage. Even the district's negotiator's eyelids were starting to droop. Finally Long concluded, "And so, if the teachers are willing to accept just Health Net, the District would see a way to finance the plan fully for employees and dependents."

Jim Tolkien leaned so far back in his chair Dee was afraid the swivel top would snap off. "So what you're telling us is that after threatening that there was no money for health care, then promising a choice of four different plans, you now are magnanimously offering to fully fund one HMO?"

Long nodded and started to clear his throat. The district's negotiator jumped in. "Jim, you know how it is. Give and take. We want teachers to be covered. This is the best we can do without charging you anything for health care."

Jim stood and placed his fingertips on the glossy cherry conference table. He leaned forward and Arthur Long shrunk back. "We'll adjourn to consider your proposal."

"Now, Dee, you know how it is with negotiations. One side asks for the moon and the other side has to act like they want to meet that request. In fact, they are darned sorry not to be able to do all those wonderful things for us deserving folk." Jim swigged some coffee in a manner which betrayed a wish for something stronger.

The six team members were spread around the small room adjacent to the negotiating room at the District headquarters. Dee and Jim were sitting together on a small couch, legs propped up on folding chairs. Dee had an ice pack to her head and was downing aspirin with her coffee.

She continued her protest. "But they had promised last time to present an offer which included four plans. We counted on that. All my figures are based upon the District spending the money that way." Dee shut up when she realized she was beginning to whine. She attributed this uncharacteristic weakness to both the events of the day and her absence from these thrilling verbal matches for over a week.

Jim reached over and squeezed her free hand. "You know how it is. Sometimes they promise things they can't deliver."

Leslie Ames, a seasoned veteran of the team, slipped into a chair beside Dee and patted her shoulder. "It's all part of the game."

Dee nodded and took a deep breath. Leslie's perfume filled her nostrils. Slowly, Dee lowered the ice pack. "What perfume is that you're wearing?" she asked Leslie.

"It's a new one from that French designer, Jacques something or the other. It's called Pink Carnations. Do you like it?"

Glimpses of the day flashed through her mind. Heidi at the plate. Broken promises. Carnations.

The pieces were starting to fit.

Chapter 31

"You want to charge into the lion's den with only your faith to protect you?" Tully shook her head at Dee. "And I thought you had given up on Catholicism."

Dee smiled. "Guess you didn't know Daniel is my middle name." She checked the last item off her list and stood. "I'm ready to plant the seeds."

"First Daniel now Johnny Appleseed," Tully muttered as she grabbed a backpack and heaved it over her shoulder. "I'll drive. You'll just make me more nervous."

The two women exited Dee's house. Just as they were climbing into the car, Dee yelped and ran into her back yard.

Cursing, Tully hurried to extricate herself from her seat belt. Before she could swing her body out of the seat, Dee trotted back, grinning.

"I forgot to turn on the sprinklers. I don't want to lose any of those new flowers."

Tully cast a wary eye on her friend before settling her bulk behind the wheel again. "Only you would think of greenery on your way to trap a murderer."

"So did you talk to that lawyer woman?"

Tully shot Dee a look. "If you mean Marsha, yes. It seems it was Steve rather than Sheila who filed for divorce, but then he never bothered to get the final papers signed." Tully snorted as she took a turn onto the Ventura freeway. "Sheila appears to have this lasting effect on her cast-off lovers, even when they know better and have every reason to hate her."

Dee wisely did not comment.

"However," Tully continued, "Steve contacted Marsha the week before Sheila died, asking for a copy of the divorce decree. Seems he was suddenly eager for closure."

"Maybe that's why he was trying to track down Sheila at the studio." Dee snapped her fingers. "Remember, he had a briefcase with him outside Sheila's. I bet he had the divorce papers with him."

Tully just grunted. She drove the speed limit all the way to Felicia's house—a sure sign to Dee that Tully still had misgivings about her proposed course of action. This contention was reinforced when Tully slid out of the driver's seat and said, "Are you sure?"

"I'm sure. I just need a few more bits of information, and this is the only way to get them." On impulse, Dee squeezed her friend tightly and said, "My faith lies in you much more than in the Almighty. Just keep that cell phone handy. If it rings, you know what to do."

Tully shook her head, but handed off the keys. Dee saw her friend in the rearview mirror, staring after her as she drove off down the road.

Dee's first stop was the Shelbourne home. The garage door was open. A black BMW and a grey Lexus were inside. She hoped that was an indication that both Mr. and Mrs. Shelbourne were at home. She noticed that the flowers evidenced neglect, as did the entire house. The white birch in the front lawn cast a shadow across the entryway. A shiver crawled up her spine as she reached for the doorbell.

"Courage, Camille," Dee said to herself as footsteps sounded inside.

Amanda Shelbourne's pale face was outlined in the crack between the double doors. Her slight smile flickered and died when she recognized Dee. "What do you want?"

"Is your husband at home? I'd like to give him a message."

Mrs. Shelbourne's voice became indignant. "You can give me the message. I doubt if Henry would like to talk with you again. He told me those lies you made up about him."

"I only told him what Sheila had in her book."

Her pale face reddened as she threw open both doors. "Sheila would never say that. Never. Henry stuck up for the girls. He smacked that boy Natalie dated in high school when he got out of line with her. Not that you care. Coming here and raking up old trash." She grabbed the doors with whitened knuckles and started to slam them.

Dee thrust her leg forward, wincing as the solid oak connected with her knee. "But you know that she blamed your husband for badgering Natalie about her grades. That's why Natalie decided to alter her transcripts."

"That's not true either!" Mrs. Shelbourne had tears in her eyes. "It was all somebody else's idea. Natalie was just left to take the blame."

Dee nodded as she headed back to the car.

Dee found a parking place on San Vicente Avenue that did not tax her parallel parking skills. Locking her trusty Hyundai, she hardened her heart and headed for the opulent entry of the Brentwood condos.

Wide black veined marble steps led to double black oak doors. A small camera mounted in the corner and a discretely disguised telephone on the side of the entry were the only clues that the interior of the wooden doors was probably steel. Dee gave a silent prayer of thanks that she was never likely to have enough money to worry about this degree of security. She pushed the numbers she had been given, announced herself, and was rewarded with a click of the door locks.

The coolness of the interior was in sharp contrast to the heat of late spring. The elevator let Dee off on the fifth floor and she almost smiled as she headed toward condo 531 knowing that one way or another this thing was going to end, and soon.

The door swung open to her knock and Curtis Lee swept his arm wide to beckon her inside.

"Rachel said you were dropping by. Said you had some things for her?"

Dee let the questioning statement hang in the air as she surveyed the living room. Azure blue curtains waved as the breeze gently pushed through the open French doors. Soft blues and purples swirled through the carpeting and were picked up in the accents in the room. From the precise color match, Dee concluded the whole effect was the result of interior designers rather than Curtis or Rachel's efforts.

"Nice effect. I bet this place is great for parties."

"Our guests have never complained."

Curtis led her to an upholstered, soft green side chair.

"I guess you must have done a lot of entertaining and behind the scenes politicking to swing that New York job for Rachel." Dee offered a smile to ease the probing.

Curtis fitted his long, thin frame into an overstuffed chair on the opposite side of the room. "Rachel sells herself. She doesn't need me to open any doors for her. Besides," he said, the corners of his mouth tight, "she isn't taking that job."

"The hell I'm not, Sweetie." Rachel bounded through the door, arms laden with packages. "I've made a serious dent in my relocation check. And this is just the start of my East Coast wardrobe. I'll have to get most of my things once I'm back there. L.A. designers just don't have the New York fashion sense." She laid dress bags over the nearest chair and placed shoeboxes on the coffee table.

Curtis' face drew tighter as the package unloading continued.

Rachel finished and flung herself on the couch. "So, Dee, did you bring Sheila's book?"

Curtis sat up straighter in his chair.

Dee nodded and tapped her briefcase. "It has some interesting things to say about people."

Silence descended.

"Really?" Rachel finally broke the ice. She raised one eyebrow.

"She sent her publisher the part that covered her mom and dad and sister and growing up in San Diego."

"And what exactly did she give you?" Curtis joined the discussion.

"All of it." Dee eyed him for a moment before continuing. "She wrote about college, winning the Balboa award, her first job. Then she had a very interesting chapter on her sister's suicide. By the way, you were mentioned in all of those." Without giving Curtis a chance to respond, Dee shifted her attention to Rachel. "Her last chapter was on her current affairs. I'm in there. So are you."

"No!" Curtis was on his feet.

"Are you trying to tell me that you didn't know your wife and Sheila were having an affair?" Dee returned her attention to Rachel. "And then there's the New York job. Sheila had that created for you."

Rachel's face grew hard and her eyes glinted. "I got that job myself. No one helped. Not Curtis. Not the network brass. And certainly not Sheila. Me." She stood.

Dee tapped her briefcase. "Then there's Curtis and the Balboa Reporting Award. That award should have been yours, right? Then you would have been in front of the cameras, not behind them."

Curtis almost smiled. "That was a long time ago and far away."

"She won. You didn't."

His smile held, but his eyes narrowed. "She cheated. Wasn't the first time. Wasn't the last."

"And then there was Natalie. Sheila was protective of Natalie."

Curtis snorted. "That's what she wanted people to think. Wasn't like that at all."

"Sheila found out you were the one who suggested Natalie could easily change grades. You even had her do yours first so that you'd end up with honors at graduation."

Curtis' check muscles flexed. "If Natalie had a scheme going, I wasn't part of it."

Ignoring Curtis's denials, Dee continued. "Sheila also suspected you had beaten Natalie several times." Curtis glowered at Dee. "You son of a—"

"You're the only son of anything I see here." Dee held up her briefcase as she walked toward the door. "Unless I get a better offer, this goes to the police tomorrow."

Chapter 32

Two paperback books, a tape recorder, several candles, a letter opener, a thickly padded manila envelope, and a baby monitor lay scattered atop Dee's newly purchased hand-carved pine coffee table. Dee sat in the corner of her second-hand blue denim couch, cushioned by two blue and red pillows. The stone fireplace opposite the couch was flanked by two new pine bookcases filled with Dee's restored books. An antique mirror hung between the bookshelves.

Rather than enjoying the serenity of her newly refurbished home, Dee was instead jotting notes and mumbling aloud. She frowned over a single sheet of paper where she had outlined a scenario of Sheila's murder.

"Too many holes still," Dee announced into the air, stretching and then running her fingers vigorously through her lengthening curls. She tossed the lined paper towards the table. It floated momentarily and then slid over the edge. She reached beside her and picked up her Peruvian rain stick. She hoped the soft clacking of the pebbles through the thorns would help her concentrate.

A creak sounded from the wooden floorboards by the kitchen. Dee stiffened. Without turning around, she said, "Knocking would have been nice, but I guess breaking in just gets to be a habit." Dee tapped the manila envelope. "I don't suppose that handing you this will mean you'll leave peacefully?"

The ensuing silence was enough of an answer for Dee. "I

know you like to vary your techniques, but I gather you don't have a gun this time or I'd be dead by now."

A flash in the mirror warned Dee to roll off of the couch seconds before the bat descended on the cushions. She pulled herself to her feet just as her assailant rounded the corner of the couch. She raised her rain stick and held it parallel to the floor as she swung around to face her attacker.

Her gaze locked with that of her assailant, Dee said, "I thought it would be you, but I kept hoping I was wrong. You see, I have this thing for redheads."

Rachel O'Neil didn't answer. Her gloved hands swung the baseball bat slowly back and forth as she assessed Dee.

Dee balanced on the balls of her feet. Then she smiled slightly and said, "If you want the book, I'll be glad to discuss an exchange with you."

Rachel gave a grim smile. "You and that damned book. I thought I was finished with it, but you had to bring back the ghosts."

"You obviously didn't find my copy when you trashed my house last week," Dee said.

Rachel waved the bat in front of Dee. "After that I figured you were lying." She frowned. "Then you show up at my apartment today knowing what was in her manuscript! So I decided to deal with you and that albatross of a book once and for all."

"Peaceful negotiations never entered your mind?"

"It will give me too much pleasure to get rid of you and destroy that book." With those words, Rachel swung the bat toward Dee's right side. Dee parried with the rain stick. The blow caused Dee's hands to sting and the stick to crack slightly.

Dee knew her rain stick would not survive a direct blow. She considered her strategy. Her back was to the fireplace. If she could distract Rachel and ease towards the door, she had a chance of creating an escape route. "I gather you're not fond of me, but I know you were more than fond of Sheila, so why kill her?" she asked as she eased her way towards the front door.

"Fond of Sheila? You might as well be fond of a rattlesnake."
Rachel shook her head slightly. "No, that's unfair to the rattlesnake. At least he warns his victims before striking. That's much more than you could ever say about Sheila." Rachel reached out with the bat towards Dee's right side. "And don't think you're heading out that door anytime soon."

Dee shrugged. "You've got a big, new job in the largest market in the U.S. How much of a victim is that?"

Rachel's eyes narrowed. "I got that job despite Sheila, not because of her. Sheila did nothing but lie to me. She said she wouldn't name names in her book, at least not in the first version. She said she'd only use pseudonyms. That night she showed me a copy. A copy that had my name throughout." Rachel slammed the tip of the bat on the floor. "She actually told me that having my name in there would increase her chances of selling the book! She had her job. She didn't care about me being ridiculed, maybe even blacklisted by the network. My fate never even entered her tiny, self-absorbed brain."

Suddenly, Rachel lashed out. Each blow drove Dee back and to the left. Her stick cracked more loudly under each strike. She lost the ground she had gained during Rachel's tirade.

Rachel feigned to the left, but Dee quickly countered with the rain stick and slid once more to the right, towards the door. The women stared at each other.

Dee held her stick out in front of her, parallel to the floor, before speaking again. "Why kill Steve Montgomery? He didn't have anything to do with the book."

"He saw me outside Sheila's apartment that day." Rachel was silent for some seconds before continuing. "I thought he saw more than that when he called me later and asked me to come over sometime and talk. There he was, getting ready for his pathetic little fishing trip. He took me back into his bedroom because he needed to finish packing. He wanted to compare notes about what we had seen. I knew that he'd bring it up to Curtis during their trip, and Curtis would know I wasn't supposed to have been anywhere near Sheila's place that day." Rachel's eyes became slightly unfocused. "He never even saw me slide the knife out of his bag."

Suppressing the memory of Steve's bloodied body, Dee brought the topic back to Sheila's murder. She tried a lie. "Sheila wrote about the two of you and how you planned your move to New York."

Rachel gave a guttural laugh. She pointed the bat straight at Dee. "We were supposed to go together. That was the plan. Both of us reporters in the largest market in the U.S. But then they dangled the anchor spot in front of her and she snatched it without a thought for me. She sold me out." The bat slammed into the floor then swung back to cover Dee who had moved a few more inches towards the door.

Rachel continued, "And there she was, with champagne and slutty get-up, all ready to celebrate her victory with you! You, not me! And she was oh so casual about it, reassuring me that a job would open for me, too. I picked up that Balboa trophy of hers and stared at it as she blithely offered me a glass of champagne. I finally realized that for Sheila it was winning that was important, first, last, and always. She beat me for that Balboa prize; she beat me with the New York job; she even beat me because I loved her much more than she loved me." Her voice hardened. "She wasn't going to beat me again."

Abruptly Rachel swung the bat at Dee's head. The rain stick shattered, but Dee was able to duck the blow. She dug into her pocket and drew out her mace. Rachel saw the move and a blow from the bat sent the canister flying.

As Rachel raised the bat yet again, Dee lunged at Rachel throwing her shoulder and the end of one half of the rain stick into Rachel's stomach. The bat smacked Dee's calves as she and Rachel hit the floor together.

Dee hung on around Rachel's middle as Rachel struggled to free herself. Rachel whipped the bat pommel-end down and bashed it on Dee's forehead.

Stunned, Dee loosened her grasp. Rachel rolled away and struggled to her feet. Dee rolled onto her back. Bending her legs, she snapped a kick directly at Rachel's knees. Rachel's scream echoed the crack of her patella as she fell writhing on the floor.

The vibration of running feet pounded into Dee's head via the wooden floorboards. Raising herself on one elbow she saw Felicia and Jenny strong-arm Rachel into a sitting position against the wall.

Tully leaned over Dee and swept gentle fingers over her forehead and cheek. "This is another fine mess you've gotten yourself into, Ollie."

Chapter 33

An hour later, Alex Pierce slid his notebook into his jacket pocket. He looked over at Dee who sat, ice bag once again on head, between Jenny and Felicia on the couch. "You'll need to come downtown and give a statement when you feel up to it."

"Only if I can bring some paint and decorating supplies with me."

Pierce actually smiled.

Gina Quinn stood talking with Tully at the far end of the living room. Seeing that her partner had finished, she rejoined the main party. "I don't suppose it would do any good to tell you that the whole operation was a damn fool idea?"

Dee smiled angelically. "I'll keep that in mind for next time."

Tully scoffed. "Next time? You couldn't even get it right this time. You were supposed to get her to confess quickly. We kept hopping around at your neighbor's house like catfish on a skillet not wanting to rush in too soon."

"Or too late," Jenny added. "Mrs. Holmes started waving her cane and urging us to battle when we heard the first crack. The baby monitor worked great, but with no video it was hard to tell what all the crashing was."

"Sorry I didn't give a play-by-play description." Dee turned to the detectives. "Will what I recorded help?"

"The recording is probably inadmissible evidence, but it's good support for everyone's statements. All that with the physical evidence should be enough for the D.A.," Gina replied.

Tully brushed her fingers across Gina's shoulder. "Will you be able to get Rachel for Dee's first assault and break-in?"

Gina nodded. "I think Rachel used the same bat today as she did the first time. There appeared to be dried blood and hair on it. If we're lucky, we'll get a match."

Pierce slid his long body onto a wicker chair and addressed himself to Dee. "She found out where you lived from Sheila's day planner. We learned that Steve and Curtis would ride motorcycles together on weekends, with Curtis borrowing Steve's Yamaha. I'm betting we'll find an extra set of keys at their condo."

Gina added, "The network bosses confirmed that Sheila and Rachel had jointly approached them about national reporting jobs. They told me they were more interested in Sheila than Rachel, but Sheila had been adamant, at least at first. When the brass decided to add a female anchor to the weekend national news, Sheila threw Rachel to the wolves in order to get the spot."

"I bet she thought it was okay since she figured the network would give Rachel her L.A. desk jockey position when she left," Felicia said.

Looking at Dee, Alex Pierce said, "You didn't even know about the double-cross over the network job, so what put you on to Rachel?"

Dee smiled wanly. "There were three things that pointed to her. One, Sheila was struck by a lefty and Rachel is left handed."

Tully interrupted. "So are about a million other people including you and both Mom and Dad Shelbourne."

"True. But the other piece was that Sheila invited me for a celebration when she was involved with Rachel. That just didn't make sense unless something was wrong between them."

Tully's snort was strong enough to ruffle the pages of a nearby magazine. "Too bad for Sheila that Rachel walked in on the big seduction scene. Sheila must have thought the herd was safely rounded up for the night what with Rachel scheduled to take her place as anchor."

Gina agreed. "When Tully suggested we check more closely on what Curtis knew and when—"

Dee's inquiring look interrupted the detective's narration.

Tully said, sheepishly, "It was after you suggested we concentrate on the unhappy couple, good buddy. I just thought I'd give our friends here a heads up."

"Anyway," Gina continued, with a sideways glance at Tully, "we learned that Curtis found out about Sheila jumping ship for New York in his morning meeting. He admitted he told Rachel before he took her off the desk and sent her out for an interview with the mayor of San Diego."

"That's what I couldn't figure out," admitted Dee. "Rachel told me she had that interview, and I didn't know how she could have driven to San Diego and back in time to kill Sheila."

Pierce cleared his throat. "Maybe she left out the part about the mayor being at LAX for a conference."

Dee tipped the ice bag in his direction. "I bet that's why you get paid for this detecting stuff! So Rachel arrived at Sheila's about the time I was supposed to."

Tully nodded. "It must have really fried Rachel's bacon to know that Sheila was taking a job without her. Finding Sheila sipping champagne and waiting for you must have been like bellows blowing hot air on a smoldering inferno."

"By the way," Jenny interrupted. "While I was making sure Rachel continued to accept our hospitality until the police arrived, she chewed me out for messing up part of her plan. Evidently she left Sheila's door ajar hoping that Dee would be the one to walk in and incriminate herself."

"She really didn't like me," Dee said.

Felicia agreed. "Just remember the dangers of being the other woman. Now then, girlfriend, you mentioned three things and you've only accounted for two."

"The third clue was carnations." At her audience's puzzled

looks, Dee explained. "When I entered Steve's apartment I smelled carnations, but there were no flowers around. Later I realized that the fragrance matched Rachel's spicy perfume. So she was probably the one who had just been in his apartment."

A rattle of metal sounded from the front door. Dee almost hit Felicia with the ice bag as she leapt from the sofa.

"Calm down, good buddy. It's just the letter carrier." Tully bent down to retrieve a twelve by fourteen manila envelope from the floor under the mail slot. She stood, staring at it for so long that Dee reached over the arm of the couch to grab it from her.

Noting the return address, Dee whistled. "Timing in life is everything," she said, handing Sheila Shelbourne's manuscript to Gina.

Chapter 34

Evie's gaze swept the living room. "It's beautiful. It's like a warm mountain cabin."

Dee glowed in the reflected praise. Especially since that was precisely the feel she wanted the room to exude. "Felicia helped me match colors, but I picked out the furniture."

"I'm impressed." Evie's look then settled on Dee's face. She frowned and tenderly reached over to trace the black, blue, red, and yellow welt on Dee's forehead.

Even the gentle touch brought a wince.

Evie drew back. "I'm so sorry. I guess it's as painful as it looks." She shoved her hands in the pockets of her Dockers. "When Tully called, I was worried. She said you were OK, but I wanted to stop by and see for myself. I'm glad you weren't hurt worse." She shook her head and pushed her glasses back up her nose. "Tully sounded a little preoccupied on the phone."

Dee grinned. "She just found out that our intrepid detective is not only newly divorced, but the David she always has to pick up turns out to be her seven-year-old son."

"That should be fun," Evie laughed. "Don't Tully and W.C. Fields have the same opinion about children?"

Dee agreed. "Which makes her continued pursuit of Gina even more remarkable."

"She said there really was a manuscript and that Sheila had sent it to you."

Dee nodded. "Book rate and with the numbers of the

address transposed. If she hadn't been cheap and inaccurate, we would have known about her network negotiations a long time ago."

"Among other things. So why did she send it to you?"

"I guess she remembered about me being the editor for the union newsletter. Maybe she wanted my help in rewriting it." Dee paused, then said with a grin, "Guess that would really be a ghost writing assignment now."

Laughing eyes met for a moment. Evie broke the contact and said, "I've got to go."

A loud, "Rrraaoo," interrupted the two women. A bundle of fur launched itself head first into Dee's leg and then rolled over to make its belly available for scratching. Dee complied with the unspoken request then made the introductions. "Evelyn Taylor, I'd like you to meet Sherwood Forrest. She's a Maine Coon cat, more or less, and one of the laziest and craziest animals I've ever met."

Sherwood rolled over, attacked Dee's shoelaces, then sprang to the coffee table as a black blur streaked into the room. The blur continued through the room, nails scraping against hardwood floor as it rounded a tight corner. Eyes wide, it came to land, four legs spread, on top of the round throw rug in front of the door.

"And this kitty is Beezlebub or BB for short. She tends to be high energy."

Evie bent down and BB, as if to negate Dee's assertion, walked calmly over to sniff her fingers. Evidently Evie's fingers passed the test, for BB then rubbed her cheeks against them. "Hello you precious thing," Evie cooed. She looked up at Dee. "And where did your furry friends come from?"

"The animal shelter. I got them yesterday. They seem to have made themselves at home."

"More like you've made a home for them." Evie gave BB one last rub and straightened. "I really do have to go."

"A date?"

"A client."

Feeling somehow relieved, Dee still didn't know what to say, she only knew she wanted to prolong Evie's visit. She considered having a relapse, but short of hitting herself, she couldn't think of how one relapsed from a head wound. Desperate, she tried, "Maybe you could come over sometime—to visit the cats? They seem to like you."

Evie smiled. "Maybe."

Then Evie leaned forward. Her warm soft lips met Dee's dry, nervous ones. Though it wasn't filled with the tingles of a first kiss, it lasted a shade too long for a goodbye. Dee let that be enough.

For now.

Other Titles Available from New Victoria Publishers

MURDER ON THE MOTHER ROAD A Mystery by Brenda Weathers
"Wit and a great sense of life's nonsensical twists and turns permeate this out-standing novel. The book is fun, funny, and wise, and features an all-time great heroine. Libby is committed to pursuing a thoroughly human path, taking on responsibility for every stray former schoolmate and pup she runs across. Mystery readers will discover endless delights in this foray along old Route 66."
 —G. Miki Hayden, Macavity winner and Edgar winner for *The Maids*
On that brilliant October day, all Libby intends is to get to Albuquerque in her sleek new motor home. On a whim she turnes off the Interstate to take Route 66, the Mother Road. When she stops for coffee at an oasis of dust and rust in a desert of sand—the Knight's Rest Motel and Café—she stum-bles across an old college sorority sister, her dead brother, and their assorted crazy relatives rushing in to claim the family fortune. Filled with delightfu-ly off-beat characters. $12.95

SUDDEN LOSS OF SERENITY A Mystery by Jacqueline Wallen
"A satisfying mystery. I was totally engaged by this slice of bohemian life in the Maryland suburbs."
Claire Winston wakes up to face a double disaster. Her teenage daughter Serenity has disappeared, and her best friend Marlene is found murdered in a nearby cemetery. Fearful that somehow the two incidents are con-nected, and that her daughter is in grave danger, Claire begins a search which leads her to the discovery that Marlene was practicing Chöd, an esoteric form of Buddhism. Is Serenity also involved with this cult? On the way to finding the killer Claire discovers how little she knew about her daughter and begins to deal with her own demons. $12.95

FOREVER PEARL—A future mystery by Claudia McKay
"...intense and compelling." —Lesbian Review of Books
"Intelligent, fun to read and holds your interest up to the last page."
The Consortium, an intergalactic East India Company, has discovered an intoxicant, pearl. Needless to say, it is in high demand. Then the supply starts disappearing. Are humans stealing the pearl, as the Consortium believes, or is the disappearance of pearl a more complex and sinister puz-zle, with answers no one wants to hear? Agent Sonya Shankar investigates and finds herself more deeply involved than she would care to admit both in the escalating disaster and with a beautiful and mysterious Contessa.
$12.95

New Victoria PO Box 27, Norwich, Vermont 05055
www.newvictoria.com